PRETTY PUG PUBLISHING

EST. 2020

Pretty Pug Publishing was founded in August 2020 by Steve Dixon.

"I started Pretty Pug because firstly I'm an author too, and being an author out there in the big wide world of publishing I know how I want to be treated. I felt that there is a complete lack of that personal touch out there.

Constantly chasing for updates and replies to your questions and just being another author on that conveyor belt of wanting to be published can make you feel unimportant.

We will reply to every question within 48 hours and will update you when we say we will. We will make you feel important, part of the Pretty Pug family - giving you a personalised plan to help get your book published."

see more at **www.prettypug.co.uk**

ISBN978-1-8384494-5-2
First published in 2021 by Pretty Pug Publishing

Pretty Pug Publishing
26 The Seed Warehouse
Poole Quay BH15 1SB

Printed in the United Kingdom by Henry Ling Limited, at the Dorset Press, Dorchester, DT1 1HD

Disclaimer: Any facts quoted or opinions expressed are those of the individual story writer and not of any organisation associated with this book.

This book has been created to raise funds 'in aid of' charity.

The producer of this book is raising funds but acting in her own capacity and not as a representative of any charity.

printing kindly sponsored by

paper kindly donated by

production kindly sponsored by

 Henry Ling Limited

1794617
Printed on Carbon Captured paper

For Mum, Dad and Derrick
I love you
I have missed you

With Thanks

I always read the acknowledgements section of a book for completeness. It wasn't until I embarked upon this venture that I had any concept of how much help and collaboration it takes to get from the inception of such an idea to the finished article.

This book has presented some challenges, as it is a collection of stories from many different contributors. I must therefore firstly thank every single person who has taken the time and made the effort to write or share their story for the purpose of helping others. In my eyes this book is your masterpiece, produced by mainly 'non-writers' who have been brave enough to share their lives. It started out as a way to raise money for four charities. It became equally important to see this through for the contributors, many of whom told me how cathartic it was to write their stories. I hope I have done you all justice. I have 'virtually' met some fascinating and insightful people through this process and would love to think that one day, we will 'actually' meet.

To everyone who wrote a dedication and donated to the book costs. Thank you, you have saved me many sleepless nights. I am so grateful for your generosity.

Thank you to my loving and supportive family here and abroad. I am hopeful that we can rebook the cancelled holidays together one of these days.

Thank you to Lu for drafting the initial press release.

Thank you Pete and Steve for your thorough and meticulous proofreading and I'm sorry if the contents were upsetting at times.

Thank you Liz for your advice and input, care and "Lizthusiasm" from start to finish.

To Jenny for your beautiful and creative botanical illustrations of the Covid-19 Virus. Thank you for literally going back to the drawing board for me.

To Luke for your amazing artistic skills. Your young mind sees things in a way mine never would.

Thank you Jo 'soul sister' for your creative eye and your expertise in finalising the press release and helping me to produce a suitable brand and logo for this project.

Andrew Diprose for introducing me to a publisher, for writing such a great cover story and following it up with genuine interest in this project.

Thank you Steve and Pretty Pug Publishing. You got it straight away, you were on board and committed from the first day. Thanks for guiding me through the last phase of this process. I wish you great success with your own venture. You deserve it.

Helen and Mark and Henry Ling Limited thank you for taking on the project, for obtaining the print and paper sponsorship and for sponsoring the book production. For your kindness and generosity in taking a novice through the final stages of book production. Helen, your emails made me cry with joy on a few Friday afternoons.

Suzy and Fiona, thank you for being my eternal sounding boards, in my life and in this project.

To Annie, honestly, you know that I couldn't have done this without you. Your editing. Your interviewing. Your modesty and your "high-handedness" (your words not mine) to ensure that the stories we selected were of a good quality. Yet, always mindful and reminding me that it was my project and my final decision. You walked with grace and kindness on this journey beside me. I am eternally grateful.

To my wonderful, ever giving sister, without whom this could not have happened. Nas, thank you for designing the website and never moaning when I asked you to change this or amend that. For being a constant supportive presence. For being my tech guru (you know its not my thing) and chief fundraiser. For being "on fire" so many Sundays. For the boundless love and generosity you exude in everything you do. I love you.

My wonderful supportive partner, Mark (Fred) you are the true constant in my life. My amazing and inspirational children Noah and Paige, your existence guides my every action and your wisdom astounds me every day.

Yassamin Amir-Ahmadi

Foreword

Yassamin Amir-Ahmadi

I had a crazy idea whilst lying awake one night. I thought of the title for a book about Covid-19 and decided to try and make this book a reality. Many people have a story to tell about their experiences in 2020 and I wanted to give them a means to do just that.

My name is Yassamin and I live in Dorset with my partner, our two children and our two dogs. I am a Pilates, Garuda and Foundation Training instructor and have a special interest in low back care. During the Covid-19 Pandemic I found myself unable to see my relatives and the clients I had looked after for many years and yet, I cared more deeply about their health and wellbeing than even before.

One day my children said to me: "Mum, we are literally living through a history GCSE question of the future!" and I realised that this unprecedented period of history will be written about and documented for future generations to study. I thought there should be an opportunity for people to tell of their own experiences of Covid-19 during 2020.

This book should become a record of what we have experienced, a reference point for future generations. Not through the eyes of a historian, but rather those of the people who lived through these times, making it a book of everyday stories in an extraordinary year. I believe this book had to be written.

I have been touched and humbled by the generosity of people, both in sharing their stories and in the way they have helped me turn my idea into reality. What has been the biggest surprise to me, and will be my enduring memory, is the strength of human spirit. Some of the stories describe previously unimaginable pain and suffering. Yet every writer has expressed optimism and the belief that life will improve again, that there will be better times.

I did not think it was going to be such a steep climb to get to this point, but it has truly been an inspirational and uplifting collaboration. Whenever I lost hope, something positive happened, strengthening my resolve to complete this journey.

From our ancestral roots, our instinct is to turn towards family and friends for support during times of illness, stress and anxiety, and fight the enemy together. This unseen enemy was different and the very nature of the virus has dictated that we have all had to endure it separately and apart.

The event we have lived through has touched virtually every living person on this planet. People have lost loved ones or fought for their own lives. The virus has created financial hardship, loneliness and isolation but, as an optimist, I believe there has been a great deal of good too. It has been a time for people to reassess their priorities, to help their neighbours or their community, to enjoy the eternal power of nature and the simple joy of owning a pet and, through doing so, enrich their own lives.

I hope these stories move you. Some may make you sad and others will make you smile. I hope many will resonate in some way. This cannot be a joyful book if it is to be an honest reflection of what we have lived through during 2020. I have sought to present a balanced collection of real stories by real people. Some of them are light-hearted and positive, and tell of small victories in a year when death and devastation have impacted so many lives.

My hope is that the profits from this book will help ease the burden of those most severely affected and of those who will need more support in the aftermath of this unbelievable year. All profits from sales of this book will therefore be donated to charities which provide support in areas of mental health, wellbeing, homelessness and hunger.

When you read these stories, please be kind and non-judgemental. Many strong opinions were expressed in these pages. They may not be the same as yours but we have all walked a different path through 2020. Every one of these pages contains someone's real experiences, their feelings and their truth.

Covid has robbed us of a year or more of 'normal' life. It has robbed us of the rituals and ceremonies we rely on to bind us as a society. It has not robbed us of our resourcefulness and determination and this book is a testament to that human spirit and endurance.

These are the stories of people like you and me. This is how we survived. This is how we thrived in 2020.

Cassidy, Savannah and Luke

For Poppy

(CONTAINS OCCASIONAL ADULT LANGUAGE)

We couldn't let Mum die alone – and we didn't. She had fought for many, many years to stay alive for us, and then, on 14th March 2020, we had to say goodbye to her. It is a date we will never forget in a year that will never be forgotten in history.

We were in the room with Mum and two other ladies who had tested positive, and in that hospital ward, my life changed forever. As Mum took her last breath, nothing could have prepared me for the pain that shot through my body. I was alone with her. My brother Robin was running dad home, because he was totally exhausted and deeply upset, but they had only been gone for a matter of moments when mum took her last breath. Every time I close my eyes, I replay the scene. So I don't close my eyes much – sleep is really difficult.

I now believe that mum testing positive was a blessing, because she went quickly, calmly and peacefully. Both dad, who is 85, and myself, 54, now have the virus, and Robin, who is 58, has just come down with a fever.

Listening out for the virus

I think I am about a week or so in, maybe four days with severe symptoms.

I can taste it, I can taste the virus in my mouth and I can hear it in my head. My eyes are sore; I keep thinking I have hairs or sand in them. My eyelids are heavy and the only things I am physically able to move right now are my fingers to type. When I close my eyes I see shapes I have never seen before – it is the strangest thing.

I see groups of triangles lit up, sharp spear-type objects shooting past my vision. One of my ears hurts as if it is listening out for the virus that is literally invading my body.

I have a chesty cough – not dry. I can feel the virus cruising through every single cell in my body but I will not let the f*****s get me. I have felt sick, my chest has hurt, I have had diarrhoea, a dry throat (I can taste the b*****d) hot and cold sweats, a fever like I've never experienced before, and now my lungs are on fire. It is hard to move, this is unlike any flu I have ever had. My mind feels clear yet muddled, my lungs and chest feel clear yet compressed. Paracetamol and inhaling steam with a little Vicks vapour feels good. I have cried so much, and I feel it isn't real; I am sure I'll wake up soon and this nightmare will be over.

Collapsed on the driveway

Now, my dad is in my son Luke's room. He is frail and weak and every time I struggle out of bed to check on him, I wonder if he has stopped breathing. A little wave of his fingers tells me he is hanging in there, but I don't think he wants to. On 23rd March, he and mum would have been married 63 years. A marriage that was so strong, the kind of marriage you can only dream about. When we called the paramedics to the house for mum, they asked her some questions to check how alert she was. They pointed at dad and asked who he was, and mum answered: 'That man is my life.'

Dad is refusing food and pain relief, and any comfort we try to give him seems futile. He can't move from the bed and we have no help.

They sent him home from the hospital in a hospital vehicle with an untrained driver; there was no other way.

The hospitals are at breaking point and at the time, they must have thought that dad was fit enough to be sent home. He collapsed on the drive. I thought he had died, and the driver was worse than useless. My daughter Savannah and Luke came rushing up to help and managed to get him in the house in the wheelchair. We didn't know what to do. Dad had a chronic stomach pain and was unable to stand, and yet we had to get him upstairs. Savannah took complete control, and between her and Luke, they managed to get him into bed. That girl deserves a medal. There are no words to describe how incredible my kids are. We managed to get Luke home from Australia literally hours before they closed the borders for six months. It is a blessing that he is with us now, to have all three of my children back together.

It pains me so much, but I know that they will soon go down with the virus as well. I pray that I will be strong enough to look after them and that my dad will pull through. I have found it difficult to give people bad news; it goes against every fibre in my body. I hope people will forgive us for not answering their messages, but I am too exhausted to talk right now. And I know that we need to keep calm and positive for the next few weeks.

We have our dogs, Joey and Jessie, plus Amber with her four adorable kittens that have been our salvation. My friends have been delivering food parcels and my fridge has never been so full. The house is full of cards and flowers and I am eternally grateful. The sun is shining, the kittens are suckling and I will beat this f****r of a virus so that I will be able to help others.

Apricots

My biggest challenge right now is my dad, the man who spent his entire life looking after my mum, seeing her through her illnesses and caring for Robin and me most of the time. He never questioned, he never faltered as a dad when we were growing up; nobody could wish for a finer man. If we needed anything, he was there, and laughter was our best medicine; he could make us laugh so much that we couldn't breathe. I remember us sitting around the table at dinnertime and dad telling me that I wouldn't be able to drink water from my glass. I thought it was an easy bet, but he made me laugh so much every time I put the glass to my lips that I couldn't take a single sip. All he said was 'apricots' and that word still makes me laugh whenever I hear it. Now this man won't accept my help. I hear my mum in my head telling me to help him, she is shouting at me, but when I try, dad shouts to leave him alone. I won't give up; I swear to God I will do everything in my power to bring that man back to health. I'll fight for him.

The house is quiet. I've been up all night. I've managed to talk to my friend, Brigitte, in Australia. She is calming and thoughtful and awake, a voice of reason and understanding.

Stay home

This is a message for everyone: stay at home and take every precaution you can. I know that we are bombarded with news and information, but if anything in my words can help even a single soul, it will be worth it.

The world is a frightening place right now, I don't need to tell you that. But what you need to hear is: please stay home. This is like nothing else I have ever experienced.

If you get it, sip warm drinks regularly and take vitamin C, zinc and magnesium, lemon and honey and paracetamol. Rest, tell the f****r it's not welcome and make a full recovery.

I am lucky. I have an incredible family. My children have been out of this world, caring for us and being so strong. I have such amazing friends, nobody could wish for better ones. Oh, this sounds like an obituary but it is not, I swear. I will fight whatever is put in front of me. I am stronger than I thought, braver than I knew and I have my mum's strength inside me. Those who knew her know that she was a force to be reckoned with.

Shreddies for Red Dwarf

And now it is morning, and I am coughing, ears ringing, feet freezing, electric blanket and heating on full. Savannah has a sore throat and I've managed to boil a kettle for her so she can inhale some steam. I believe this virus doesn't like heat. The other two, Cassidy and Luke, are sleeping.

A small breakthrough: I changed tactics with dad. This morning I went to his room and told him that I know he is a smart man, so he must realise that if he doesn't eat, he won't have the strength to watch Red Dwarf. He agreed to a small amount of warm Shreddies, the first thing he has eaten since he came out of hospital. He is like a skeleton, frail and weak. My dad, Tai Chi Master and the fittest 85-year old I have ever known.

I spoke to my friend Jane whose husband is stuck in South Africa; they've closed the borders and won't allow him out. The locals are beating up the English and Europeans, blaming them for bringing the virus into their country. It is a war, a war where we can't see the enemy.

If you have the strength, call old friends, call new friends, speak to family members you haven't spoken to for a while, make amends instead of fighting. Let this bring us closer together as a nation. Be thoughtful and understanding of each other's needs. We are all struggling in our own way, so think before you say anything that may upset people who are only trying to help. Take it from me: helping someone with the Corona virus when I have the virus myself is a testament to my own strength. Who would have thought I could do it....

On Mothers' day, my daughter gave me a card: 'It's okay.' I don't know why it's okay, but I feel calm. It may be the giant bottle of Baileys that Savannah managed to find on a shelf. Or maybe it is just the fact that I loved my mum each and every day that she breathed. She is within me, she is helping me fight and she will always be by my side.

Artwork by Luke Gevell

Hugs

I've begun to appreciate my friends, the countryside, the smell of the farmyard and, more than anything, I've begun to appreciate all that I have to give; to someone, the community, my friends, my family, everyone that knows me. I just need a hug to prove it's all worthwhile, just a hug to know we are all connected once again.

Trevor

Nineteen

01

Questions

What is protection from infectious disease that occurs when a sufficient percentage of the population has become immune to that disease?

(ANSWERS IN BACK OF BOOK)

The Cuddle Curtain

This cuddle curtain was created by 14 year old Sam Duncalf in order that he could hug his grandparents at Christmas.

For all the non-believers

My first experience with Covid was when I was coming towards the end of a nine-day stay in hospital. It was just at the beginning of lockdown, and suddenly, in the middle of the night, about 20 medical staff came to our ward and started doing all sorts of tests on a little old lady before taking her away with suspected Covid. I guess that because at that point it was all so new and unknown, all the medical students who were on shift had come to observe. At one point they brought a mobile X-ray machine into the small ward, it sounded like a road sweeper coming past my bed. The lady was taken away to an isolation bed and the masked cleaners came in to do a deep clean everything at 2 o'clock in the morning. Myself and the other lady in the small ward then had to wait a few days to find out if the lady taken away had tested positive to know if we were safe or not. It was a long few days.

More recently, when I was taken into hospital again with a recurring infection, it was far, far worse. I had been brought to the Emergency Department by ambulance, and I had to wait all day on a trolley because there simply weren't any beds available on the wards. Everybody there was lovely, but it was a long, scary wait. In the end, I was lucky enough to get a private room – by then I was terrified that I would get Covid from being on a ward so I was really grateful that the first available bed was a private one. After three days I was allowed home because the antibiotics had done their work. I still had to wait for the paperwork and the medication, but they needed my bed so they told me they were very sorry, but I'd have to wait in reception. As soon as I left my bed, they cleaned it, and I watched the next patient being brought in. At moments like that, you realise how serious the situation is. So I sat in reception, huddled in a blanket, waiting to go home. And yes, I was scared.

I had reasons to be terrified. During that stay in hospital, a person I knew well was in there as well – on a ventilator. He had previously been in to be treated for cellulitis and was sent home again, but he had caught Covid during his hospital stay and had to go back in to be put on a ventilator. A few weeks later he died in that hospital. It hits you hard when someone you know actually dies. I also heard stories from a consultant friend of mine, who usually doesn't work on the ward, but worked there now because it was so busy. He could go into a normal ward one day and three people would turn out to be positive after all. Then the next day, one of them would have died and some more would have tested positive. It made my own regular hospital visits scary experiences

Suddenly, Covid was everywhere. One day, my opposite neighbour was taken away in an ambulance, on oxygen. He came home again, but a week later, he was taken away again, and not much later yet another ambulance arrived to take away his wife. The ambulances got to know the way to our street quite well.

The narrowest escape I had was when my son, who still lives at home, caught Covid. My husband had bought us all our own thermometers and one day my son woke up with an aching back. A friend of his had had Covid so he knew that it could be one of the symptoms. He took his temperature, and phoned me from his loft bedroom to say he needed to get tested. He was positive... We managed to isolate him; we put a table outside his room to bring him food and drinks, and kept ourselves well away. Although he's only 18, he was really very poorly. Covid doesn't seem to care about young or old, thin or fat, and even being very careful doesn't always seem good enough, because I have no idea how he could have got it. He's fine now, thankfully. But I've heard stories from a friend who is involved in a study about long Covid and it is surprising how many young people and children suffer long-term consequences. We've been lucky that my son came off lightly.

It makes me so furious when people deny how serious all this is. I read stories on Facebook where people rant and rave against vaccinations and deny that there is a pandemic at all, and it makes my blood boil. Covid has had such an incredible impact on so many people's lives. A while ago, a friend of mine who is a nurse came knocking at my door and when I opened it, she burst into tears. She lives on her own and she desperately needed to talk to someone, so she had driven several miles up to my house. She told me how incredibly tough it was, how the hospital was full to the brim, how a normal ward had been turned into a Covid assessment ward to catch the overspill. She told me how hard it was to watch the patients suffer, and how terrified she was to get ill herself - how it sometimes was more than she could stand. This was at the time when you weren't allowed to meet up, so I made her a cup of tea, put a chair outside on our sun porch and sat there with her, talking, until she calmed down. People walking past frowned at us, and I wanted to shout that they shouldn't judge, they had no idea what this woman was going through. Covid has brought out the best in some people, but the worst in others.

One day, we will look back on all this and I wonder what we will make of it all. But I know that the fear I have felt was very real – it still is, even though I've had my first vaccination - and even when things are back to relatively normal, I don't think I will forget how I've felt. Just as I won't forget how lovely the NHS staff have been through it all.

Angela

Nineteen

02

Questions

What is government enforced confinement of people to their homes except for necessary work, exercise and essential shopping?

(ANSWERS IN BACK OF BOOK)

An ode to Covid

I lived through the war, as others before
We had bomb shelters, schools, doodlebugs and strict rules
But Covid has ripped all those memories away
No contact, no kissing, no hugs, so much missing
Beautiful grandchildren, faces on Zoom
Another world now, delivering gloom
Mental health issues, a problem ahead
Hard to keep positive, when you are fed
Bad news every day as you lie in your bed
Stay home, see no one, no choir, no friends
Where will it go, when will it end?
iPad's and iPhone's help time pass away
But waking up knowing there's no fun today
Drains your resolve, you just have to pray
Keep going, keep smiling, have click and collect
The vaccine will save us, our lives to protect......

Jill - 80 years

In dedication

To all those who stepped out of their usual lives and normal roles to selflessly provide extraordinary and difficult medical, practical and emotional care to many affected by Covid-19

Jenny

"My husband carrying Aubrey out in the car seat. In the background, you see a big sign with information about Covid. It's a very special photo, because it tells the story of our daughter's start in life."

Call the midwife

Having my first baby in Covid times was definitely not how I had expected it to be. Being pregnant felt quite lonely, in a way: except for two scans, my husband couldn't be with me during my appointments, so I had to do it pretty much on my own. It was sad that he could not be as involved in the pregnancy as he would have wanted. I desperately missed my family as well – some of them I didn't see at all during the whole pregnancy, except on Facetime. The second lockdown, after Christmas, was the hardest. I was stuck at home, and only went out for hospital appointments and for walks around my own neighbourhood.

It was also quite scary: before the pregnancy I was low-risk for Covid, but when you're pregnant you're suddenly in the at-risk category. I was worried; what would happen if I caught it? It's supposed to be a joyful time, and it was, of course, but it could have been so much nicer. I couldn't have a normal baby shower with my friends and family, so we had it on Zoom, but it's not the same, and since it was my first pregnancy I would have liked to go to classes and meet other mothers-to-be. I missed out on all that.

I'm a midwife, and as soon as I knew I was pregnant they took me out of clinical practice and gave me an admin role, so I didn't have to be around anyone who might be infected. I don't think I ever looked after anyone with Covid; at the very beginning there were some ladies who were at risk, but nothing came of it. I stayed in my job until I was 36 weeks pregnant, but from 30 weeks onwards I worked from home. It felt like an extra protection that I didn't have to go in and out of the hospital and the office.

The birth was lovely, though, and one of my friends from work looked after me. I was used to seeing people in masks and PPE so it didn't upset me, but I can imagine that it could be quite scary for women in labour who didn't know what to expect. Because of Covid, I could have only one birth partner – my husband – but under normal circumstances I would have liked my mum to be there as well. No visitors were allowed except for my husband, but in a way it was nice to have that time with our little girl to ourselves instead of loads of people trying to come and see us. And Aubrey was a lovely healthy baby, which was the main thing of course.

I stayed in hospital for just over 24 hours for the birth, but a couple of days later there were complications and I had to go into another hospital. It was only for one night and the baby stayed with me, but it was frustrating. We had just got settled at home, and now we had to go through the whole thing again: the Covid swabs, my husband waiting for his test results and not being able to be with me… It felt wrong: you're just trying to work out how to do things at home with the baby, and then you have to go back in. But everybody there was lovely and we were well looked after.

My husband had a couple of weeks' paternity leave and he now works from home. It feels good: he can spend time with his daughter and he's a great help to me. In a way, it makes up for the lonely moments during the pregnancy. Aubrey doesn't like to be put in her Moses basket; she prefers to be held all the time, so my husband cuddles her and I can get dressed and have a shower. The things you took for granted before, like having a shower, suddenly become an achievement when you have a baby. Strange: however much advice I have given to new mothers as a midwife, when it comes to your own baby, you're not really prepared. But I just love it, and I love having my husband around. I just feel sorry for my mum; she would have been here so much more in normal times.

Aubrey is now eight weeks old, and hopefully things will slowly get back to normal. I look forward to seeing the family, for them to see her, and in the summer we will have a little party to celebrate her being here. I can't wait to take her to classes and meet other mums, and I long to be out and about with her. Before Covid, everybody's life was so busy. We've had to slow down and appreciate what we've got. In the future I will make the most of seeing the family. Just to go for a walk and spend time together will be wonderful. Nothing extravagant or expensive – I will just enjoy the things we took for granted for so long.

I have a picture of when we left the hospital, with my husband carrying Aubrey out in the car seat. In the background, you see a big sign with information about Covid. It's a very special photo, because it tells the story of our daughter's start in life.

I can't wait...

As soon as I can, I shall go shopping for new clothes and I will have my hair cut and I might restore the blonde colour.

I can't wait for restrictions to lift so that I can go out to a cafe to have hot chocolate.

I can't wait for sunshine,
I can't wait to see my friends,
I can't wait for my brother to come home at weekends,
I can't wait to see the children in my local school, I help them with reading.
I can't wait to use my new car lots and lots,
I can't wait for life to happen again.   **JLB**

Covid-19: A child's view

WHAT IS CORONA VIRUS AND HOW DOES IT MAKE YOU FEEL?

I didnt have it so i dont know
Cameron, 7

sad sad sad and ill,
Felix, 8

Corona virus is a virus that can effect old people and I feel very worried
Dylan, 8

fine because ive had it
Charlie, 8

covid is the strongest virus yet
Dylan, 8

sad lonely

Covid Botanical illustration
by Jenny Malcolm

Today, we mourned you differently

Today, we mourned you differently –
not in the way we would have liked to or felt you deserved.
A fettered celebration, not enough to even begin to pay
tribute to the life you've lived.

Today, we mourned you differently –
the pageantry was sparse,
we had no singer to sing your songs,
and the shoulders of the fine men you reared were bare –
they would have gladly though sadly
taken your weight with pride,
and carried you to where you now sleep.

Today, we mourned you differently –
your friends and neighbours lined the street –
a noble gesture but poor substitute
for the squeeze of a shoulder,
an embrace, and the vice-grip handshakes full of grief,
solidarity and questions.

Today we mourned you differently –
the bare handful of us,
the chosen few, stood around you,
while broad-backed men from the old days trembled in the
distance,
and from a parked car, your brother looked on with pursed
lips through the condensation.

Today, we mourned you differently –
sad eyes looked up
from where big hands were holding little hands that didn't
understand-
not that the big hands understood much better.

Today, we mourned you differently –
but this much is true – you are gone,
but not without a trace,
as you are in every face you leave behind,
in every imprint of your foot on the path
you so diligently wore from the rose bushes
to the kitchen door.

Today, we mourned you differently.

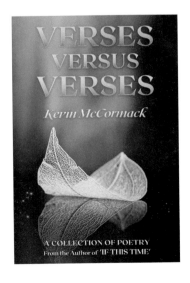

Poem included with the
kind permission of
Kevin McCormack
from his poetry collection
Verses Versus Verses.

The juggler

In the centre of our town, on a corner of the street, I often see a young man juggling fire sticks to make some money. 'Homeless but trying', a little cardboard sign says, and nearby sits a pile of sleeping bags and other possessions. There's sometimes a cup of coffee as well, or a sandwich, because people like him and occasionally give him food. Today, when I walk past, he is juggling some wooden sticks and the cardboard sign says that someone has – ironically – set fire to his fire sticks. I ask him what happened. "A little while ago, a friend came to me in the middle of the night because his partner had chucked him out. It was 3 a.m. and he was scared, because there was lots of noise on the street and he'd never been homeless before. I made him a bed and gave him a blanket, my last bit of food, and my only spare boxers and a pair of socks, just so that he'd be okay. He seemed fine; not happy of course, but not really depressed. I went to the toilet and when I came back there were fire engines everywhere. My friend told me he'd fallen asleep with a cigarette in his mouth, but a security camera from the bank nearby showed what had really happened. He had got out of bed, poured white spirit over the blanket, got back into the bed and set it alight. He had wanted to commit suicide. He was fine, only his jacket was scorched and his phone had melted, but all my possessions were burned. I haven't seen him around since; he hasn't come to tell me how he is or even to say sorry. I don't care about the stuff, except my fire sticks, but I'm worried about him. So now I'm juggling wooden sticks because I don't like just sitting there. It's not the same though."

Homeless during Covid

Daniel is 25 and he has been homeless since he was 13. "My parents died when I was young, and I was an only child, as were both my parents, so I had nobody. I was put in a care home, but it was really bad there; there was a lot of abuse, they locked kids in cupboards and so on. So I've been on the streets ever since, and I sleep in the corner where I do my juggling, even on nights when it is bitterly cold. St. Mungo's has housed about 400 people in B&Bs, and only one or two of us on the street are actually homeless. There is a big difference between the homeless and the beggars who have somewhere to sleep.

You can tell by the stuff they carry – I have two sleeping bags – and by how dirty their hands are, because when you're really homeless, you don't have a place to wash."

I ask him if life is harder for him in Covid times. "I didn't even know about Covid until the police told me that juggling my fire sticks during lockdown was in breach of my liability insurance. We were a month into the pandemic by then, but because I have no access to the news, I didn't really know what was going on. But yes, it's been a lot harder to earn any money; there are far fewer people around. The homeless charities have been very good though. I have been tested for Covid – you have to be tested before you get put up in a hotel anyway – and I actually don't know anybody who has Covid. Maybe it's because we are in the fresh air; that's safer than in houses with heating and air conditioning."

He spends the odd night in a bed & breakfast when he has the money. "There used to be shelters where you could get a bed for £ 3.50 a night, but they have all been changed into HMOs – Houses in Multiple Occupation, where people rent a room. So it's a B&B or nothing. But it is hard for me to be inside now; I get claustrophobic because I'm so used to being outside. When I go to a B&B, I arrive late at night, and leave early in the morning, and I need to have all the windows open, and make myself a little bed on the floor. It's like being institutionalised when you are in jail; I've been conditioned to live on the streets."

The soup kitchen on hold

I ask him how people can help, and he talks about the charities that bring food and clothes, and an old couple who have ordered new fire sticks for him online. "Feeding yourself is expensive when you're on the street. You can buy a burger for a pound, but I am tall and I have a fast metabolism and it doesn't keep you going for very long. Or you can buy a meal deal in a Tesco Express, but that's an expensive way of eating. You can't go to a big supermarket, because they think you're stealing, and you can't buy a cooker because it would be stolen in no time and the police would take it away anyway. The soup kitchen is only open twice a week now, because of Covid. So when people buy food for me, it helps."

He adds: "But sometimes, it is nice when someone just comes up to me and has a chat. It's good when somebody shakes your hand and listens to you. The worst thing is when people just ignore you and act as if you are invisible. We're normal people, and everyone is just one step away from living on the street, especially in these uncertain days.

There are times when I think prison could be a solution: you get a roof over your head, three meals a day, and no worries. Prison would save me, in a way, but I don't want to do any of the things you need to do to go to jail. I don't want to steal, and I don't want to hurt anybody."

When I walk on, he picks up his sticks and starts juggling. And I think of the irony of this Covid world, where we are scared to go outside and hide in our comfortable houses, while there, on the corner, a juggler stands who owns nothing, and sometimes dreams of prison.

Daniel is 25 and he has been homeless since he was 13

Simple pleasures

Lockdown was an opportunity to do some amazing things in your local area that you just never get the chance to do during "normal" day to day living. Life is busy and taking some time to yourself is amazingly productive and empowering. Just doing what you want to do when you want to do it and not having calls on your time from others is not selfish it's what we all need and lockdown has highlighted this in so many ways. I took the opportunity in the glorious weather, we were fortunate to have, to see the sunrise at our local beach on a number of occasions and how spectacular was that.

The expectation of a new day and what it has to hold and the excitement of what it might bring is exhilarating. Listening to the sound of the never ending relaxing waves as they lap against the shore gives your mind the opportunity to stop and just live in the moment. When do we get these opportunities to love the simple natural pleasures in life – we have to grab them with both hands when these opportunities arise and that's certainly something that I have taken from this unprecedented year - grab every opportunity and make the most of the simple things in life. Some friends have said why get up so early but seriously it's so worth it. Enjoy these natural never ending delights that we have at our fingertips. Aren't we lucky...

AJD (7th April 2021)

Furloughed

Food for thought

When I was furloughed, made redundant and suddenly out of work at 55, I couldn't see myself finding a new opportunity in the middle of a pandemic any time soon. But I was wrong and after 30 years of working in the corporate sector I now manage a local food bank on behalf of a Christian charity.

Ours is not a 'donations' kind of food bank. We raise funds via government grants, which allows us to buy the food and personally deliver parcels to recipients. This is good from two points of view: we offer fresh fruit and vegetables (not just the dried goods) and when we deliver, we try and stop to talk to the recipients, building relationships and finding out what other needs they might have. Call it signposting, community, whatever – but we call it love. Our food bank brand is 'Love Your Neighbour'. One of the people we deliver food to is a man in his thirties. I'd like to tell you what has happened to him in the last year.

The chef's story

 "During the first lockdown I worked some five months without pay – I had started at a date when I had just missed the furlough arrangement the government had set. I was a head chef – I am 36 and have over 20 years' experience as a chef - and had decided to move back to Dorset to be closer to my family. Then, during the second lockdown in November, the place I worked at had to close, which meant I lost my job and my live-in room. I tried to find places to stay, but shortly before Christmas I ended up on the street. My mum had died a few years before, at 51, and by now, my stepdad had throat cancer and didn't have long to live.

I had always been too proud to ask for help, but in the end, I hit rock bottom and I was desperate. On Christmas Eve I rang my friend Pete with what little charge was left in my phone and prayed he'd pick up. I knew Pete and his family from church. He was always there for me as a brother in faith and a friend who cared. Without hesitation he booked me into a hotel and gave me the food I so desperately needed. Shortly after this, Bournemouth Council put me up in a hotel. This sounds swish, but it's not. It's temporary accommodation for people like me: one room and a microwave. I am not even allowed to cook in the hotel kitchen for Health & Safety reasons.

Through various organisations and churches, Lovechurch 'Love Your neighbour' got in touch and organised to deliver weekly food boxes to me. I never just got the food in a brown box with my name on it; it always had my name and a heart on it. This gave me the sense that I wasn't just receiving food, but that there were still people out there who knew about me - Christian or not, there were people who cared. 'Now that I, your Lord and teacher, have washed your feet, you also should wash one another's feet' says John 13:14. I interpret this as: pay the kindness forward, because we all need help.

When I'm not in a kitchen, I suffer with depression, and sadly my step-dad has recently joined my mum. But a brown box of food with a heart on it goes a long way towards making me feel better."

It could happen to anybody

I myself have lived a charmed life, and have had very little exposure to deprivation, let alone any understanding of the causes of poverty. So what have I learned from running a food bank during covid19?

- To stop making assumptions
- To stop treating the poor as fundamentally different from other people
- To realise that it could happen to me

According to the Trussell Trust, there has been a 61% increase in the use of food banks in the last 12 months. With unemployment predicted on a scale not seen since the early nineties, there will be further rises in poverty. By the end of 2021, over 700,000 additional people will be classed as destitute, meaning they cannot afford essentials such as housing, energy and food. This is on top of the year-on-year rises in the number of people unable to afford food and forced to use food banks across the UK.

Birth – the year of change

I'm not sure I can really put into words what working as a midwife through a pandemic has felt like.

Naively, considering the history of Britain and the fact that a previous pandemic was just over 100 years ago, I would never have thought that I would have to experience something like this. I think back to a year ago (March 2020) when I was wearing a mask for the first time to take a patient for a specialist scan. It felt strange walking through A&E, seeing everyone sitting at a distance from each other and feeling the fear in the room. A year on it's our new normal. We spring into action for an emergency, dressed top to toe in PPE, and don't bat an eyelid at how far from normality this really is. It has felt like a year of constant change. As we have learnt more and more about this virus, we have had to constantly adapt so that maternity care could continue.

What hasn't changed is the way we keep women and babies safe at such a special time in their lives. Maternity cannot pause and wait, it has continued and what feels like a baby boom is now in full force!

The long night shifts in full PPE, hot, sweaty and thirsty, were tough and often scary. It was new and unknown to us, but we put our fears behind us and just carried on with the job. Everything else was still the same; we still cheered women on and encouraged them when they felt like they couldn't go on. We were still there every step of the way. It felt strange and unnatural to pass a mother their new born baby while I was dressed top to toe in PPE, a tight fitting mask and steamed up visor hiding my smile as I congratulated them on the birth of their child. The moment, still full of love and amazement at what women can achieve, was tainted by Covid-19.

One day it dawned on me how impersonal the PPE made the experience feel; the mothers wouldn't even recognise me if I met them again. A year on and this somehow feels almost normal.

Only a couple of months into this new way of working and my

hands became cracked and were bleeding from excessive hand washing. This meant a week off work for my hands to recover, which filled me with so much guilt for not being at work. A year in now and the mask acne is real. Wearing a surgical mask for 13 hours a day is my new normal.

Something I've noticed as a midwife is how much we use our body language and smile when caring for women, and I feel the mask really gets in the way of this. The emotional side of coping with the increased demands at work is taking its toll. I am tired and drained and the end doesn't feel in sight.

I'm fortunate to work at a trust where everyone picks each other up. We continue to laugh and be there for one another, day in day out. Everyone so easily adapts to new rules, new ways of working, the shortness of staff who also have to isolate, staff who are redeployed and the daily changes. The days are long and working during a pandemic is not how we envisioned our midwifery careers to be, but we keep going.

Yet what I'll remember most is the sense of teamwork, how quickly this has become the new normal, how we have adapted everything we do to ensure the mothers and babies are still safe.

New life continues to be created, despite the fears and the sadness of so much life ending. We carry on. Thousands of babies are born every day and we are there to ensure that the women feel safe and have the experience they deserve. We feel their sadness and disappointment when they can't have their two birth partners with them, we are aware of the feeling of isolation this creates at what should be the most exciting time. We understand the emotions women feel coming to appointments alone, hearing their baby's heartbeat for the first time alone, the first ultrasound alone, with no hand to hold.

But throughout all this, we've constantly been there for them, and we have taken on that extra support role to help women feel they're not alone, and to empower them every step of the way.

Despite working full time, and in spite of the pandemic, we set ourselves the challenge to raise £1,000 to improve our pool room facilities for women on the labour ward. We set individual goals, so that as a team, we could walk the distance from the Princess Ann Hospital in Southampton to the furthest hospital in Scotland. Through socially distanced walks on our days off we walked a total of 2,500 miles and managed to raise over £10,000!

I feel extremely proud to be a midwife at a time when constant changes have been made to improve the maternity care we provide. It has been an invaluable experience to see first hand how a service can adapt so quickly to ensure that we are there for women, at a time when people everywhere are advised to stay apart.

The 12 tiers of covid

ON THE 12TH TIER OF COVID, MY BORIS SENT TO ME...

CHRISTMAS IS CANCELLED!
DON'T FORGET BREXIT!
10PM CURFEW!
LOCK-UP THE STUDENTS!
NHS IN CRISIS!
TRACK N TRACE DISASTER!
RULE OF 6 CONFUSION
HANDS!   FACE!   SPACE!
PANIC BUYING LOO-ROLL
3 MONTHS OF FURLOUGH
2 METRE DISTANCE

(BIG FINISH HERE PLEASE!)

AND A FREE EYE-TEST AT BARNARD CASTLE!

(AND AGAIN!)

AND A FREE EYE-TEST AT BARNARD CASTLE!

In dedication

For the workers &
The working from home-ers,
For the friends of Wray and the friends of Nephew,
For those away from home,
For the sharers,
The vodka drinkers &
The popping to the shop-ers.
For those who couldn't have any,
For the underage-ers,
The bbqer's &
The wine at 11am-ers.
For those who frequented the "Pabbling Pool",
For the new lovers and those who shared love at a distance.
For the joy, the chuckles and the love,
All experienced and stationed at 244, lockdown 1.0

Grandchildren

"I desperately miss my grandchildren. I see my grandson of nearly five on Facetime and he remembers me, but my granddaughter is now 15 months old and I'm worried that she wouldn't even know me if she saw me. It's been a year since I touched them and I have missed so much of their lives already."

Shirley

Nineteen

03

Questions

What is the name of the first conferencing app that started with video as it's foundation?

(ANSWERS IN BACK OF BOOK)

Don't forget the students

There is something I need to say, as a parent, as a teacher, a mentor, a human being.

Today I heard that the son of a friend of mine has ended his own life. It is the third suicide I have been confronted with during this academic year. They all have something in common: they all concern sixth-form students. Young people who weren't seen as a priority during the past year. Students who haven't been able to celebrate their last days at school, who haven't been able to go anywhere, who have lost out on education. Their future has been compromised before it even began.

There are those who say that these young people have nothing to complain about. Their need is just a drop in the ocean of life. But what is it really like, when your life has been reduced to studying, when you have to sit at your screen alone all the time, trying to do your work? When your dreams have been put on hold and friendships fall by the wayside?

I don't want to go as far as blaming Covid and the lockdowns for the irreversible decision each of these young people has made. But when you don't feel good in your own skin, a lonely existence at the computer certainly doesn't help.

In a while, I'm going to hug my three children. It's all I have. This week, I am going to phone my students again. A short conversation with a tutor who wants to know how you are; maybe it helps a bit. And I am going to approach the pupil who is sitting on his own in a corner of the playground, staring ahead.

So whether you come to school to talk to the teachers, or are a teacher yourself… take the wellbeing of the students seriously. They are having a hard time. And for some, that little bit of attention may just make the difference. I hope so. I, for one, am going to try. As a parent, as a teacher, as a mentor, as a human being.

Tom Debraekeleer

The invisible virus

In-viris-able...

in its peregrination
duplicitous in its stealth
equivocal as a wink

disputing immune defence
dissembling as an idea
the virus wanders casually

quiet as rat in drainpipe
behind skirtings, along rafters,

our virus scuttles
on its invisible course

softly we breath it
easy as Spring air

numb to its welcome
fools to its presence,

the virus is master
we its pleasure-dome
it shuns our lockdown
free to float and find

re-discover your hermit
know him, like him
only he will save you
your long lost hermit

abandoned at birth
the one, the only one
to outwit a virus
to bring everyone
crowd-light again.

Thank You, Michael Sherman 04/2020

This poem was introduced by Gill Kaye Editor of Ingenue Arts and Culture Magazine www.ingenuemagazine.co.uk

And used with kind permission of Michael Sherman

"I do"

I do, I do, I do

My partner Joff and I had been together for over eight years and any time we spoke about getting married, we said that 2020 would be the year. After getting engaged we found our venue and set a date in October - wedding planning had officially started!

When the global pandemic hit in the March of 2020 , we didn't really know what to expect - like the rest of the world. We had six months until the wedding and we were optimistic that everything would be over and we'd still be able to go ahead as planned. Lockdown eased and we sent invitations to some 80 people; we were adamant to go ahead, although the family were more sceptical. As the date drew closer, we started to realise that they had been right. Weddings were going ahead with only 30 people and it didn't look like it was going to increase.

We sat down and drew up a list of 30 people. It was hard, and it was even worse to have to tell people they were no longer invited. We decided on our immediate family and closest friends: our parents, our grandparents and our siblings – without their partners, a handful of closest friends. We had always planned for our godchildren and a niece to be the pageboy and flower girls, so they were still coming with only one parent each. It was tough, but everybody was incredibly understanding and felt for us instead of being annoyed they couldn't come.

I had my hen-do locally with just the bridesmaids, which they made so special, and Joff was going to have his low-key stag-do the night before the wedding with his groomsmen (more of a night in with the boys!). We had been to our food tasting, I had one more dress fitting to go, we'd bought all that we needed and were pretty much ready to get married! The excitement was starting to build that we might actually be able to make it happen!

September 22nd, 2020 - three weeks and two days to go: the government announced weddings would be cut to 15 people only. We could only laugh.

Wine and a whiteboard

The announcement was at lunchtime. We called each other, laughed a lot, mainly in shock, and decided we'd discuss further after work. We got home, sat at the table with a bottle of wine and a whiteboard. It was so hard: the venue we had booked hadn't decided what they were going to do, and we had to look at all our options. Should we postpone the whole thing? Was the venue we had paid for a waste of money for only 15 people? Should we go ahead and have the wedding somewhere else and use the venue next year for a party?

The rules had changed so many times, and we constantly had to adapt to what could be done. The 15 people in the wedding party included us, but not the 'working' people such as the photographer. We were allowed a sit-down meal as a reception, but nothing else. We phoned a couple of country houses in the forest to see if we could hire out their restaurants for the reception, saving our venue for a party down the line. If we had the meal in a restaurant, we couldn't all sit at one big table; we'd have to have tables of six –rather awkward when you're 15 in all, and no-one could guarantee those tables would be together. At least the other punters would get dinner and a show! Then there was the 22:00 curfew. The ceremony was always going to start at 16:00, at Ringwood Parish Church. It didn't leave that much time for the rest of the day, but it didn't really matter, since all we could have was a meal. The obvious choice was to make the meal the main event – and make it big! A few days later, we had a phone call from our incredible, supportive venue Sopley Mill who gave us the option to have both our wedding on the planned date and have a party for the one year anniversary! We decided to definitely go ahead: the whole year had been so bad for everyone, we had barely seen each other and we all needed something joyous. Although it may sound morbid, but with Covid taking so many lives we didn't want to risk postponing. We were having our 2020 wedding!

We got the list out again, and made some really difficult decisions. There were so many people close to us whom we couldn't invite. In the end we came up with the guest list. Our parents, our grandparents, my brother who would give me away and our bridesmaids and groomsmen. Joff's younger sister was one of my bridesmaids, but the other siblings couldn't come, the flower girls and pageboy couldn't be included either. It was just our immediate family and the bridal party.

Everybody was very disappointed, but we decided to fully embrace everything Covid-19 had thrown at us and live streamed the wedding so that people could still see us get married. One of my closest friends, whom I've known since we were in nappies, has a media company, so we paid him for live streaming and to create a video of the whole day. Which meant that he could be there as well!

Two days before the wedding, Joff received a phone call from one of his best men, Paul, who was in the Navy. One of the contractors working on board his ship had tested positive for Covid. Yet another speed bump in the wedding plan! Cue a rapid fire PCR test and 2 days of waiting...

Stavanna and Joff

Here comes the bride

We did almost everything ourselves with help from some very talented friends. Bouquets were made by a close family friend, I made the cakes, and one of the bridesmaids and I made a lot of the decorations for the venue. It was a perfect opportunity to spend some time together after months on video calls, which was really special.

I got ready at my nan's house and because only six people at a time were allowed in the house, we had to do some juggling. One of the bridesmaids, my sister-in-law to be, did our make up, the sister of another bridesmaid did our hair and when she left the photographer could arrive.

We drove to the church and when I got out of the car, I had the most wonderful surprise. Many of the friends and family that we hadn't been able to invite, were waiting for us there. I looked over at my friends and burst into tears - it didn't make for very flattering photos but really special memories.

The church is stunning; I had a very long walk down the aisle and at the end, I was greeted by a handful of treasured people. We had decided not to get married in the main church, but in the chancel. The guests sat where the choir members usually sit and the wonderful Reverend allowed us to sit in the Sanctuary. It was really intimate and simply beautiful, with the huge stained-glass windows behind us. It didn't feel empty at all. Everybody did have to wear masks, except for Joff and I, but with groomsmen in black suits and the bridesmaids in burgundy, simple black masks didn't ruin the look at all.

After the ceremony we had some time to walk around the grounds, and talk to all the people who were still waiting there; the sun was shining and the love and happiness we felt was beyond anything we imagined it to be. It just so happened that some celebratory fizz was available to takeaway from the church too – with enough to spare to go around everyone there.

A magical meal

We were the first to arrive at Sopley Mill and just the two of us had a bit of time to ourselves, to have a drink, and have photos taken in the sunset. When the guests arrived shortly after, we had some seated welcome drinks outside, a few more photos and a socially distanced bouquet throw – even Joff's Grandma got involved, who's over 80!

The meal was on the top floor of the old mill, which can only be described as show-stopping. We had wanted to make it extra special for our small party and the caterer, Molecular Magic, exceeded all expectations. He is not only a chef, but a chemist and a magician who makes every dish look spectacular. There was lots of dry ice, and sometimes what you saw was not at all what you would taste. Everyone was in awe of the food.

Paul, the best man, didn't get his test result back in time. He hadn't been able to attend. The other 2 best men had set up the room so he could do his speech virtually, in full naval uniform. It was sad and amazing all at the same time, but we made the best of a bad situation once again.

It reached 21:30 and we realised we still had a cake to cut and a first dance to do. We cut the cake and it was put in little bags to take home, and we went downstairs for the traditional first dance. There was time for one more song: Wonderwall, and that was it. The day came to a sudden end, but it was truly amazing... It was so special: we got to speak to everybody on a personal level and everyone enjoyed themselves; the room just radiated joy.

Molecular Magic

Such a perfect day

For our honeymoon we had planned to go travelling, but with no chance of that happening in the near future, we decided to explore the UK instead. We hired a campervan and travelled around Devon and Cornwall. The weather was glorious, just like on our wedding day. We had managed to choose the only sunny week in October that year, and made the absolute most of everything we could.

On reflection, we decided not to go ahead with the one year anniversary party that we had initially planned. The wedding was so incredible and we feared we'd be constantly comparing the two days: Something so special came out of such a sad and stressful year. I didn't think we'd be able to duplicate the happiness of that wonderful day.

The guests welcome the happy couple at Sopley Mill

Lockdown

Goodness me, waking up to the reality of not going to cheer on the mighty AFC Bournemouth – unheard of.
Not going out to buy another shirt, to sit alongside all the others that have not been put into service yet.
Booking a holiday that has a major chance of not happening.
Going out dressed like a bank robber and daily news updates of families torn apart by a virus escalating due to
the actions of selfish people.
Believing this disease is a scam and Big Brother is controlling us.
Sad just listening to people of all ages having to deal with Long Covid and life-changing conditions.
Missing close family –precious time which can never be made up.
Every day groundhog day – no variety or
anything to look forward to.

Post Lockdown

The good thing to come from lockdown is having time to reflect on simple things we take for granted.
Thinking of others less fortunate than ourselves
Appreciating each other more.
Feeling inwardly rewarded for helping – which should be the norm, not enforced by a cruel epidemic.
Lastly, true friends and how we have missed them. Sharing a problem and making one another smile and laugh.
Do we need to see a top show or just sit and chat and have a drink whilst watching the sunset.
Long may some of the lockdown changes remain.

Nineteen

04

Questions

What is the term for an outbreak of an infectious disease on a global level?

(ANSWERS IN BACK OF BOOK)

Staying strong

Some people have spent lockdown learning to bake sourdough bread. Others made sure they walked 10,000 steps a day, and yet others became Netflix addicts. James and Jack did it differently: they decided to open a brand new gym.

"This is our third year of owning our own business as personal trainers," says James. "We started out seeing some 30 people a week, and we wanted to expand. We wanted to reach out to more people, coaching, improving mental health. We wanted to create a welcoming place.

During the first lockdowns we kept going with online work, we did Zoom sessions, quizzes... Most of our members continued to work with us, and the days went quickly; eight hours on the computer went by like nothing. We also helped Dorset Mind with their June 500 challenges: we got members into running clubs, we did a mini biathlon, mindfulness challenges, hydration challenges...

In the meantime we kept looking for a location for a new bigger gym. We came across this place through sheer luck. The building was far too big, so we approached a coffee shop about opening a branch within the building. To our surprise they said yes. We then found a barber, and then created a space for massages and treatments too. When we got the keys on December 2nd, we were convinced that there would be no more lockdowns. We started to make the space exactly what we wanted: a warm, light open place with loads of artwork. No egos, no mirrors – we found that people don't particularly like looking at themselves – and no phones. Gyms can be intimidating, but we tried to make ours welcoming.

When the news came of another lockdown in December, it was like a kick in the teeth. We put down our paintbrushes and had a few beers, but we never really allowed ourselves to get too discouraged.

In January we were doing 60 -70 one-to-one sessions a week to keep people motivated, as well as Zoom sessions. From March, we were allowed to do group sessions outside, which we held in the car park. And yes, we sometimes got soaked in the rain, but you have to be resilient. Being resilient is the key to everything for me. And somehow I feel that Covid brought us closer together. After an initial dip, our membership nearly doubled since Covid started."

James

The team at eMotion Fitness hub

Bringing People Together

On April 12th we were ready to move inside our eMotion Fitness Hub. We are very hands-on and we wear many hats: we do coaching and sales calls as well as the cleaning! There are seven of us here. Jack and I are co-owners, and we have three coaches and a fulltime P.T., a mix of men and women. We don't segregate the classes on gender or ability; everybody who wants to work hard is welcome here. We work in small groups of six people for our P.T. training sessions and classes, and we offer anything from circuit training, metabolic conditioning, aerial yoga and cardio to Farmstrong.

One of our pillars is education, so nutrition is part of that. We have a six-week programme in the form of videos and teach members how to write their own eating plans, in such a way that they can actually keep it up. Once you have the principle, you can adapt the method to your life. People who have a problem or an injury can do one to one training until they are ready for the group session; they need a more tailored approach.

Now that we're finally here, I feel as if it hasn't really sunk in yet. Yes, it's hard work and I hope that in the future, we can afford to have a day off work every now and then. And of course it has been quite terrifying to make such a big investment in these strange times. But we did it, and we still have great plans for the future.

What if there is another lockdown? Then we'll adapt, and go online again, and work outside. The main thing is that we want to bring people together, give them a space where they like to come, where they can work on their health and strength and be away from day-to-day worries for a bit. As it says on one of the texts on our wall: almost everything will work again if you unplug it for a few minutes - including you.

Almost everything will work again if you unplug it for a few minutes...

Including you

05

Questions

What is the term for a government job retention scheme which enables employees a leave of absence with a percentage of their normal wage covered?

(ANSWERS IN BACK OF BOOK)

Lockdown lust

It was a day in May, I can still hear him say
Come to the island, come play
Be with me, maybe you'll stay

My head said "No" you should stay at home
My heart said "Go" you're longing to roam
The wheels started turning as I started my car
The adventure began, to the island a far

I was leaving my home feeling mild trepidation
My heart pounding hard, full of joy and elation
The world was in lockdown, on my own life was tough
In his presence stood passion, would one day be enough

I arrived on the ferry, such a glorious day
His strong figure waiting, no time to delay
Heading out to the hills, there was no looking back
It was lust and desire, it felt true, it was fact

As we lay in the sun admiring the view
We kissed and caressed, we kicked off our shoes
I longed that this day would never end
As we drove round the island, every beach, every bend

I loved being with him, his laughter his smile
My thoughts and desire lived for a while
I try to remember so the lust does not fade
My passion now lies where memories are made

My body on fire, a million words still to say
Left craving another magical day
When time stood still and nature basked in its glory
Creating a perfect end to my story

I'm missing his touch, I still feel his skin
Endless dreams, I long to feel him within

The Lock-Up.

A friend of mine asked me if I would write a
few pages about being on my own during
Lock-Down or (Lock-Up) because it makes you
feel like a prisoner doing Solitary Confindment,
when you are in a flat on tour own.

   I am not in a nursing home, a Care-home, I
am in my own flat in a block that they say is
Warden assisted, it is very nice here but they
are very strict and wont let anyone in, and
they are'nt very keen om you going out.but I8m
afraid I do, even though there is a shop
down-stairs, there a lot of things I need that
they don't sell. I really behaved myself for a
couple of weeks, then I had to go to Tesco's
to get some money out of the wall as my bank
had closed and I needed some money to pay for
my Carer Nida. As I looked into Tesco, there
was'nt a soul there, so I went in and did my
shopping, they had done so much, to protect
everyone you could'nt have been safer in a hospital
so from then on at least I could do my shopping,
it was'nt much, but at least it made me go out.
I was at the stage I was finding excuses not to
go out, I knew this had to stop, so what could I do?

I knew I had to do something, or I would be
talking to the house-plants befor long. I was
as deaf as a post, could hardley see, certainly
could'nt run the minute mile, but happily
my memory was very good, a lot of my friends
had said I should write a book about my life,
I had thought a lot about it, but untill the
lock-down had never had time befor. It has taken
me all summer, and have nearly finished it
now. (it is certaánhlya good way to pass the time)
but at my age "nearly 94, there's a lot to put
in it.

If Olivetti still have a factory, and
they are still making typwriterd and they have a
room where thej show all their typwriters from
day one, till the latest modles today, tell them
there is one here, between 65 and 70 years old,
and with the right tapes, and someone who can
type, it works perfictally.

When I started with this typwriter if
anything could go wrong "it did", firstly
I had to throw lots of paper away plus about 12
ribbens.
Took about 2 hours to put a new ribben in and nonstop
swearing all the time.
Had to take it into the garden for Yossi to fix
it when it stopped.
Dropped one of the main screws into the works,
and nearly threw it out of the window, wasted about
a week trying to get it out, I then knew it was
me not the machine, I had totally forgoten how
to use it. When I finally "cracked it" I suddenly
realized that half the lock-down had passed, so
wanting to write this book I had to get going.
I finally finished the book just befor the
lock-down ended, it certainly made the time fly.

Here I am nearly 94, and if it had'nt
been for the typwriter, I would have spent a lot
of lonely hours watching T.V. and waiting to die,
but I am too busy now, so I think this typwriter
has saved my life, and certainly...
..... MY SANITY ....
Anyway, writing the book made me think
of a lot of things. I know they have'nt tested
the vacine on children yet, buutasssoonnas they
do, I think they should be done as soon as
possible, firstly, They are our future.
secondly, They could go back to school without
their parents being worried that they might
catch this virus (they would be a lot better
in school than running around a super-market
without any protection) because their mother
has to shop for food and has no one at home to
look after them. in a few cases it means that
they get a good lunch every day.

Not being any good at Science (or much else) this
lock-down has taught me something, you don'nt
uasually catch anything unless you are close
to somebody who has it, what proved it to me was,
(this was befor Covit-19) It was the General
Election, I had just got rid of my car and taken
delevery of my Buggy, I was very pleased with it,
and because I could vote at the Church (just up
the road) I descided to go on my Buggy. Well it
did'nt just rain, the heavens opened, and the
voting place was in a shed at the back of the church,
by the time I found it I was soaked, there was
no one outside (because of the rain) so I did'nt
want to leave my new buggy there either.

I managed to get into the shed but knocked most
of the signs down, after I had voted, they helped
me turn the buggy around and out of the shed
befor they put the signs back up. That went well,
so I thought as I was wet anyway I would go on to
Tesco to do some shopping, "I managed that without
doing any damage"I was amazed how kind the
motorist were when I left, they stopped and let me
go through, they must have thought I was some kind
of nut, driving my buggy in those conditions,
anyway I got back to the flat entrance, but because
it was wet it was also very slipery. so down I
went in the entrance. they are not allowed to help
you get up, but as I could'nt manage it on my own
they had to bend the rulls and help me as no one
could get in or out of the building as I was blocking
the entrance. Finally I got into my flat thinking
there was nothing else that could happen, only to
find when I went into the kitchen I had left the deep-
freeze door open for hours, (things always happen
to me in threes) this is nothing to do with the
Virus. I did'nt come into contact with anyone for
quite a few days after that, and did'nt catch a cold
after being so wet and cold, it was'nt too long after
that we had th-is "Lock Down" and I did'nt speak to
anyone "except on the phone". I, who was used to
catching 3 or 4 colds a year, (I could catch a
cold from someone who was in the same room as me
not even sitting close,)so distance must be important.

We are fighting a war, a silent invisable war, if
I did'nt know differently, I would think the little
"Green Men" from space, were trying to take the
world over, anyway we have to beat it.
If I did'nt catch a cold in over a year "at my age"
and believe me I tried, I went out in all weathers,
freesing cold, wet or dry, and not even a sneeze,
but I hardly came into contact with anyone, so
social distance must be the answer.

Sadly, last year, brought many a tear,
It's hard to obey, but please do as they say.

Keep all you're friends, and when this nightmare ends,
Lets pray we kick COVID away.

.....Keep Social Distance.....

. . . .

P.S. It works.

Viv and the Olivetti

In dedication

A Fantastic account of a remarkable life led by a remarkable woman.
I am proud to be able to call myself her son.

Jameson Lee

The silly President

I read my daughter a wonderfully funny fairytale last night. It was called 'The President and the Bad Illness'.

Once upon a time...

 There was a mean and silly President. One day, a bad illness came to his land. It started to make people very sick and many died. Instead of telling the people to stay at home and be careful while he would do everything possible to fix it, he told them that the bad illness would fly away and everything would be okay. He was so mean and silly that even when all the doctors and scientists told him he needed to do something he didn't listen and he said to the people: "Don't listen to them, everything will be fine".

Unfortunately the bad illness didn't fly away and more people got sick and died. So instead of telling the people he was very sorry, that he was wrong and he would now fix it, he told them it wasn't his fault: he had done the best that anyone could do and the illness was caused by the evil wizard Chynna. He went on to say the evil wizard Chynna was so naughty that he made this illness to give his land a booboo* and should be put on the naughty step.

The silly President was so worried that people would not like him, that he told them to use the magic liquid Clorox to make the bad illness go away. That didn't work and it made people worse. So in desperation he got his best friends the Foxes to spread the news that the evil wizard Chynna had planned to use this illness to make Chynna's land the most powerful in the whole wide world, and that he would destroy the President's land. This way he thought his people would hate Chynna and love him because he was protecting his land.

Now in the President's land there were two types of people: those who were very silly and believed everything the President told them and those who were sensible and did not believe the President. The sensible people thought: "Hold on, this President has lied to us before and even if the evil wizard Chynna did send this illness on purpose, why didn't the President do something about it when it first arrived? Does this President not care about this land and the people? Is he not capable of looking after us? Why did he not believe the doctors and scientists; did he think he knew more than them? He did seem to be a very mean and silly President and maybe he should go on the naughty step!"

And so it came to pass that the bad illness did not fly away, more people got sick and died and the land got a huge booboo. Eventually some of the very silly people decided to be clever and not believe the President anymore. Finally they all put the President on the naughty step forever!

And they all lived happily ever after   **The End**

*Booboo - child's term for injury

Nineteen

06

Questions

What is the term for a government scheme aimed at boosting the economy whereby restaurants are subsidised to offer half price food during weekdays for a limited period?

(ANSWERS IN BACK OF BOOK)

How William Shakespeare is helping his community through Covid

William Shakespeare has become a great help in our community throughout lockdown 2020. I don't mean the brilliant bearded bard, though his sonnets have soothed me late into lockdown nights when I cannot sleep. No, I mean the bearded collie crossed with a labrador - our William Shakespeare Billington-Beardsley.

This five year old bundle of energy goes on duty outside our house every day. A sign invites people to pat our friendly pooch - with a gloved hand - if they prefer. And many do. Some days, there is a socially distanced queue as people wait to enjoy Will's warm welcome. Recently, a cyclist stopped for a cuddle. She then sat on our garden wall and wept. "I live on my own and Will is the first living being I've touched since lockdown" she told me through tears.

A single mum with a daughter with special needs pays a regular visit. "Will gives our day structure and helps my daughter make sense of these restricted surroundings. Thank you so much!" Parents stop with their kids and take selfies - Will has more fans on Facebook than his owners! And he is showered with doggie treats and gifts left in his basket on our driveway.

He's a welcome break we are told by one mum with two toddlers in tow. He's the bribe at the end of torturous home schooling. And if Will is not there, - we need our pet therapy please is the cry! There have even been Will Wars! Little Isla who lives round the corner has grown so fond of Will and he of her that she walks him most days now. But now there is also Ellie from a neighbouring road to fit into his walking schedule. And a lovely chap called Richard who said Will has made such a difference to his mental well being in the past few months.

And if we are honest, William Shakespeare is being shared, not because we are kind but because we decided to paint our kitchen during lockdown and didn't want his black coat looking more like a badger!

Will Shakespeare

I'M VERY FRIENDLY
(UNLESS YOU HAPPEN TO BE A CAT)
I'M ALSO COMPLETELY
CORONAVRUS FREE.
GIVE ME A PAT AND
IT'LL KEEP YOU CHEERFUL.
I'LL ENJOY IT TOO!
WILL (IAM SHAKESPEARE)
THE DOG

Who could resist a pat?

But how often he reminds us of the power of touch. I watch the warmth of contact from my dining room window as Will twerks his entire body in delight as visitors come to say hello. He doesn't do social distancing. I envy how close he gets to my friends and neighbours. People approach him with open arms like greeting an old friend, the same people that nervously step aside from me. And just for a few moments, the sound of laughter fills our silent street and there is a sense of normality again.

With apologies to the original William Shakespeare and Henry V, " A little touch of Will in the day"... it certainly seems to go a long way in lockdown.

And Will continues to share the love now - in fact he is so booked up for walks that as his owners we rarely walk him! The power of touch, the power of sharing, the power of pets - thank you Will.

Will Shakespeare 'on duty'

The prison that Covid created

Being away from Family
And having Covid – I don't wish that on anybody.
I've missed my nephews growing up -
I've been shielding for more than a year now.
I feel enough is enough.
In a care home environment you are isolated.
Being in your own room, 14 days at a time.
It's not easy being on your own, with no one to talk to, especially
when you have anxiety. It's like a prison.
Especially in a care home. We are restricted and can't go out.
We've been here for over a year – with two Easters in lockdown.
And my 40th birthday. Will my next birthday be in lockdown?
I'm so frustrated with Covid.
The World doesn't know what it's doing.
Everyone should have the vaccine and they need to wear their
masks, otherwise we will never get back to normality.
We don't know the truth... Will we ever?
How will we remember the people that have passed?
And also the people who have fought through Covid, like myself.
I feel tired all the time, no energy.
When will my taste buds get back to normal?
In a care home with a disability, I've lived through Covid.
Covid is still taking its toll.

Nineteen

07

Questions

What is the term for the ability to resist illness when exposed to a disease?

(ANSWERS IN BACK OF BOOK)

My mad mother

A Short Story - A Long Memory

My mother, Hazel, was 89 years of age. She lived in a small room in a psychiatric ward for patients detained under the Mental Health Act. She was 30 years or more older than the other residents. Normally people of her age with her problems mellow out with age and no longer need to be detained. Hazel was not like other mentally ill people of her age. She was still fiery and furious, so her needs were deemed best met in a traditional psychiatric hospital. She had no friends, she had severed all ties with her two children, my brother and me, and she had never met my children. Hazel had no home. She had never been to a funeral. Her room had no pictures, no photos, just 3 suitcases stacked on a partially empty cupboard.

Hazel was born in 1930, a Londoner and wartime evacuee. She had been afflicted with episodes of madness for as long as I remember. Her diagnosis generates fear in the 'normal population': Paranoid Schizophrenia. It was a long time before we fully understood it.

Her final episode started around her 65th year and never ended. Human rights laws govern mental health services. The person cannot be forcibly treated 'unless a danger to themselves or others'. Hazel disturbed the peace. She frightened neighbours. She could be dangerous. Once she tried to set fire to a carpet in her block of flats to rid it of a rat infestation. There were no rats. That was when we tried to get help but we failed. She was not considered dangerous enough for treatment. So, she spent 17 years homeless, living the life of a nomad, travelling from country to country, town to town, staying for a short time in cheap hotels and motels and then moving on when paranoid and delusional thoughts overwhelmed her. Twice she was forcibly detained and hospitalised and then released. Finally, in 2013 she was detained and never released. We always believed that had she got the help she needed earlier things would have been different.

In March 2020, my brother and I got news she had contracted Covid-19. Miraculously, she recovered and was returned to the Psychiatric Hospital. We expected nothing less. She was as strong as an ox and we were proud. When she returned, she was confined to her room and she stopped walking. Movement was her lease of life. She walked daily for hours and hours so when she stopped she started dying. Still she refused to see us. She believed we would be in danger if she did. Finally, she no longer had the capacity to refuse and I got a phone call telling me she would soon die. I drove the 140 miles from Dorset to Northampton to see her.

I hadn't seen her for over 10 years. She lay deathly still, a tiny, skinny ghost of her former self, taking her last gasps of life. Her illness was a cancer of the mind; she had been hateful, spiteful and cruel, yet her final moments were so gentle. The soft thwack, thwacking of a tennis ball as Wimbledon played quietly on the TV, the rasping of her breath; two goldfinches in flight passing her window. I told her what I needed to say. I held her as she took her final breath, like a seed wafting away. It was peaceful and final. I kissed her. I hadn't kissed her for 20 years or more. She was warm and soapy fresh, her skin was soft. It was a lovely kiss. The nurses hugged me and fed me and told me stories about my mother that made them smile. They told me she was a 'lady'. Lady of the manor. Requesting food at mealtimes with a 'please' and a 'thank you'. Aloof, distant, grandiose. She was important. The nurses loved her for it. She livened up those moments that were otherwise dull. These nurses were truly good people. I was humbled. I felt safe. I shall never, never forget them.

And so it was that Hazel passed away in a mental hospital on 4th July, American Independence Day. She loved America, dreamed of going back to America and died on one of America's most important days. She spent the last seven years of her life confined, plotting to escape back to America where she had spent much of her life. July 4th 2020 was a fitting day for her death.

A life ends, but we carry on. There were things to do: arranging for the body to be collected, sorting out death certificates, funeral arrangements, forms and signatures, telephone calls, trawling through papers. She was leaving her three suitcases and money to the Pope. Pope Benedict V. She was not a catholic, she mocked religion, she saluted Donald Trump. But if you climb inside her mind for a moment, you will understand. Her mind was wrecked with delusions and paranoia. She was being pursued by a depraved religious cult. Her children were in danger. Her money was in danger. Who better than the Pope to protect her? Her children would be left alone and her money would be safe. It makes perfect sense doesn't it?

Hazel was Covid collateral, a statistic.

Her memory lives on and her story has not quite ended. She didn't choose her mental illness. Eventually it possessed her mind. She was from humble origins, an only child born in London. She was different. She was a free spirit. She had travelled the world. In her twenties she lived in Denmark and Paris and cycled and hitchhiked across Europe. Later she met her husband-to-be, my father, whilst working in Nigeria and they lived for a short while in Iran, the UK and finally the U.S. She flitted between the UK and US for many years. Her final mad adventure in her 80's, was travelling around Spain, France, Italy and Mexico. Hazel was quirky and clever. She was fiercely independent, single minded and brave. She loved the theatre and read the Sunday spread-sheet cover to cover. She was cultured and lively. She was funny with a furious drive to survive. Hazel was my mad mother. She was loved. She is free.

By Penny
written with respect to people experiencing
mental illness before and during the Covid Pandemic.

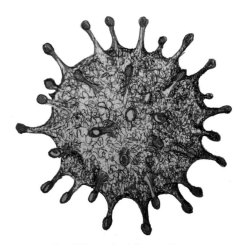

Covid Botanical illustration
by Jenny Malcolm

Covid-19: A child's view

WHAT ADVICE WOULD YOU GIVE TO SOMEONE WHO IS WORRIED ABOUT CORONA VIRUS?

~~you will be gine.~~ Aurelia, 8

Just stay sage and soshal distarce. Hattie, 8

they can always talk to me. Mabel, 8

keep calm Oli, 7

Think about the positive side like spending with samily. Lilly, 10

Holly, 12 I'd say to stay calm and think about the posetives and if you are worried don't be shy to talk to someone as it could really help.

keep hands to your self + space. and were a mask and keep at home Dylan, 8

Nineteen

08

Questions

What is the much overused word we have heard in 2020 for something that has never happened or existed in the past?

(ANSWERS IN BACK OF BOOK)

Vivienne's perspective

Vivienne Pringle - masked up on the underground

I was inspired to write this on the 21st January 2021. On that day 38,905 new cases of Covid were confirmed and 1,820 deaths were recorded in the UK.

These were the worst daily statistics since the start of the pandemic in March 2020.

115,000 people in the UK and over 2 million people in the world have now died from Covid over that period.

What follows is my account of how I felt on that day and my reflections on the year that led to these salutary milestones.

Vivienne Pringle

January 2021 – the second wave and the third lockdown

When I am watching films or television programmes of large gatherings of people being close to each other I am beginning to feel that it's a dream that might never become a reality again.

We no longer see any of our family or friends in person. The Government regulations say that you can meet up with one other person who is from a different household outside but it's impossible to maintain the required 2 metres of social distancing whilst walking the London streets.

I am 65 and Hamish is 69. We are lucky to be in good health, but we have heard of too many people like ourselves succumb to horrible symptoms and worse. So, we are being very careful.

Hamish goes up and down our stairs 25 times for his daily exercise (he claims to have done multiple ascents of Everest!). I do an online stretch class 2 or 3 days a week with my favourite teacher, Alison.

Vivienne and Hamish - and their lockdown exercising

I also go for walks and bike rides. Richmond Park is a favourite as you can get away from other people there.

It is interesting to think about how we have adapted to the new normal. I continue to do a lot of paperwork and admin for me, Hamish, Macmillan and my mum. And the occasional watercolour and acrylic painting which I started in the first lockdown. Hamish is the first to admit that enforced isolation suits him as he can pursue his new career as a full-time artist without interruption...

I play on-line bridge with friends about two or three times a week, have WhatsApp chats with friends and family as well as Zoom suppers where we sit and eat with our computer on the table.

Lockdown artistry

It is hard not to talk about the dangers and worries of Covid in these chats. But this is broken up by comparing notes on the latest box sets on Netflix, All 4 and Prime. Current favourites include 'Lupin', 'Call my Agent' and 'Delhi Crime'.

A ray of hope is that we are beginning to hear about friends who have received the vaccine. We are hoping that ours will come by the end of March. Currently there are worries about whether the Government's decision to delay the second dose of the Pfizer and Oxford vaccines is the right one.

I read in the paper this week that 15% of people who have had a positive Covid test carry on working. And only one in four people who have been exposed to the virus self-isolate for the required 10 days.

I am sure many of these people are carrying on working for financial reasons. But this must be contributing to the devastating rates of infections and deaths that we are recording as a nation.

This week Glastonbury was cancelled for the second year running. The Olympics in Japan are due to be postponed again. Ski resorts are to remain closed for the rest of the season.

On Thursday a minister said '… it is far too early to book a summer holiday'. Is our family holiday booked last September to Club Med in Turkey in early June in jeopardy?

Having said all this, we know we are so lucky compared with most people.

My heart breaks when I read about how the NHS professionals are working so hard and being stretched beyond their limits.

My brother David, a GP, was meant to retire at the end of March last year. Instead, he set up the UK's first Covid hot hub to diagnose whether Covid sufferers need to be transferred to hospital. His hub is currently open until 10pm every night and he is exhausted.

My nephew, Robbie, is an A & E doctor in London and is even treating patients inside the ambulances that are queuing up outside because his hospital is too full. Here is Robbie talking about Covid on the BBC. Another interesting, perhaps ironic outcome of these strange times is that these two doctors have been under the most stress of their careers, but both feel it has also been the most interesting and stimulating period of their professional lives. They both had Covid late last year.

This is a photograph of our two-month-old nephew who was hospitalised two weeks ago with Covid. Luckily, he recovered well and is now home again. Frightening times while Boris tries to navigate the disaster that we are going through.

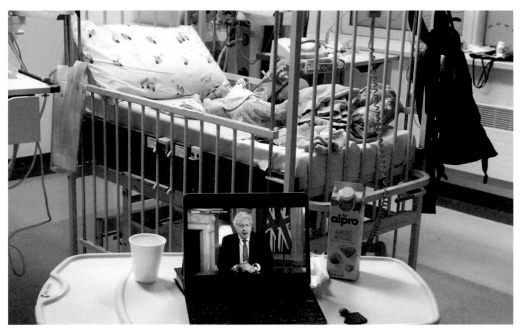

Covid didn't just affect the elderly

London, post pandemic, may look and feel a little different but there are lessons that must be learned. The lack of planes in the sky is literally a breath of fresh air. The effects of pollution are being reversed. The need to meet the climate change targets is getting a lot more airtime. Sales of new cars have plummeted and the message of buying 'green' is finally being heard.

What will Oxford Street and other local high streets look like? What will replace all the department stores that have gone to the wall? It will be fascinating to watch as whole new markets will undoubtedly appear for these spaces but who will occupy the empty skyscrapers in the City?

I am amazed at how quickly the concept of working from home (WFH) has been accepted by so many employers as the way forward after the pandemic is under control. Twitter announced in the middle of last year that none of their employees would ever have to go back into an office again.

I think the pandemic has managed to achieve something that I would never have thought possible in my lifetime. Working parents of young and school age children will be able to work flexibly from home without the fear of jeopardising their careers. Genuine sharing of home and childcare responsibilities seems to be more possible. Will people flock back to their expensive gyms or will they carry on with their online versions?

Some businesses have stormed ahead during lockdown – Amazon, food delivery services, online fashion and homewares to name just a few. But the hospitality and event industries have really suffered. As soon as we are able, I feel we have a collective responsibility to go out and spend in these places. Hopefully, the Government's furlough initiative will have saved a fair number.

Planning ahead is still looking very difficult. Travel will continue to be tricky until the vast majority of the world is vaccinated. Daily reports of new strains of the virus continue to worry us – will the current vaccines combat the South African and South American variants? Time will tell. And time hasn't been on our side during the pandemic. Many decisions have had to be made at breakneck speed. Some have been right, and some have not.

History will be our judge.

Memories of the first wave and first lockdown: March to June 2020

From mid-March I ran the gauntlet of the empty roads to take food to my 96-year-old mother's house in Surrey. I would take photographs of the food in the back of the car so I could explain my journey to the police if they stopped me on the way home! We could only meet her outside for most of the year. But we were so lucky she wasn't in a care home where we wouldn't have been able to see her at all.

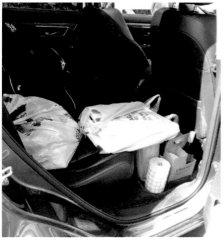

Shopping through the Covid lockdown   Socially distanced but precious times outside

In May I went for a bike ride through central London. It was a beautiful sunny day, and the streets were deserted. I was literally the only person in Oxford Street at 11am on a Saturday morning. Tears streamed down my face for seeing London and all it has to offer never looking more beautiful. But more tears were shed for the lack of vibrancy that shoppers, tourists and office workers bring to central London. This isn't what I signed up for when I decided to live in London over 40 years ago.

But I am confident that the London that I love so much will return – albeit differently – and better...?

A moving memory from the first lockdown was the clapping for carers outside our houses every Thursday evening and all the children's drawings of rainbows in windows all over the country showing their support for the NHS.

An unexpected bonus of this was a coming together with our neighbours and the formation of a Gainsborough Road WhatsApp group which has harnessed a lovely community spirit which will continue well after the pandemic is over.

Hamish finished his MFA at Wimbledon last June. Sadly, the whole course went online-only for the last term and his Final Show was cancelled. But a few lucky students had a piece of their work selected for 'London Grads Now' at the Saatchi Gallery which showcased students from the top 6 London art colleges. His 'Lockdown' work gained much deserved publicity.

Our 4 children's Covid experiences

The deserted streets of London

We are very lucky that 3 out of our 4 children are still in employment and have been able to work from home, while the fourth is self-employed and can work anywhere.

Benedict, our second son, Kirstie and their two young children were bubbling with us in November for 6 weeks whilst they were between houses.

Working from home sounds easy but it was interesting to watch Benedict disappearing into the spare room upstairs before 8am and then reappearing at 7pm having been on Zoom calls all day. Most days he would hardly make it downstairs for a cup of coffee and eat a hastily made sandwich. He says he is working harder than he has ever done before without even the exercise of walking to the tube to go to work.

He had to work from his kitchen table at the same time as Kirstie whilst having to look after 2-year-old Stella. They used to have to take it in turns to work from 6am – 10pm. Thank goodness Kirstie was pregnant with Kit so she could stop working when her maternity leave started in June.

Here is a photograph of a drive by visit in the first lockdown.

Lockdown drive-by

Kit's arrival on 3rd July was the highlight of the year. Luckily Benedict was able to be in the hospital for his birth. So many fathers weren't. Well done Kirstie for working so hard during the whole pandemic to juggle everything and everyone as well as moving house.

Arabella, our daughter, works for a tech company based in massive new offices in Old Street. She has been told that it is very unlikely that she will need to return for more than two days a week. She does miss the camaraderie of her office but feels that the opportunity to choose between working at the office or at home will also bring great benefits.

Bella and Alex, her boyfriend, have had a very disrupted year too. The Covid outbreak started while they were working and living in Paris. After these headlines they decided to make a break back to England for lockdown.

Unfortunately, they caught Covid on the Eurostar back to England in the middle of March. They were both quite ill – Bella had some breathing difficulties and Alex lost his sense of taste and smell.

They were lucky enough to spend the 9 weeks of the first lockdown in Sussex with Alex's family. But sadly, they also managed to give it to Alex's mum and brother too. When they recovered, they were able to go on some lovely seaside walks. I managed to go down and see Bella once before she returned to Paris and we enjoyed a gorgeous socially distanced chat on the sea wall in Emsworth.

Tristan our third son, moved into a 2 bedroom flat with Lara in October. Because they are both working from home a one bed flat just wouldn't have been big enough.

Should employers be contributing to the cost of home working??

However, homeworking has also meant savings on commuting and takeaway coffees and lunches so perhaps things are evening out? Tristan works for an exciting start up that has invented a domestic recycling machine. Let's hope it comes to fruition as the amount of plastic waste that is being used by the home food delivery companies that have proliferated in lockdown is just horrendous.

Masks have become the norm even on the Itchenor ferry!

Tristan spent Christmas with Lara, her parents and her brothers. One of the brothers came home from university with the virus but was asymptomatic so didn't realise. Amazingly no-one else in their Christmas bubble caught it.

Sebastian, our eldest son, went on holiday to Columbia in January 2020 ... and hasn't come back. He is in a band that tours the world doing festivals so there hasn't been much call for that in the last 12 months! His life out there appears very much removed from our own and he is enjoying beautiful weather in a glorious seaside location.

Who can blame him for staying?

Despite a rather dodgy internet connection he stays in touch with us and is busy writing new songs.

He also caught the virus despite being in lockdown in a beach hostel. His remedy was to fast for a few days!

A very sad end to a very sad year

At the end of November my mother died of a non Covid illness in her own bed with my brother and I by her side.

Only a fortnight beforehand she had been in hospital and we couldn't visit her because of Covid. Being able to return home was such a blessing and gave her family the chance to see her. The thought of her dying on her own in hospital would have been too horrible.

But so many people have.

Here she is a couple of months before she died. As stoical and resilient as ever. She will be missed so much.

Mum - may she Rest in Peace

Fortunately, we were allowed to have 30 people at her funeral followed by a socially distanced mulled wine wake outside her house in the freezing cold.

Postscript: Monday 8th February 2021

I am having my vaccine today! The NHS has risen magnificently to the challenge of vaccinating as many of the over 65's as quickly as possible. Over 12 million people have been vaccinated since just before Christmas. I never thought I would get mine as soon as this. I didn't mind queuing outside in the snow for half an hour! Ironically, we are currently enjoying being a leader in the world for Covid vaccinations rather than our normal position of being a leader in the world for Covid deaths.

As Hamish and I were given different vaccines from each other it will be interesting to see how we fare over the next few months whilst we try and avoid any new strains that come our way.

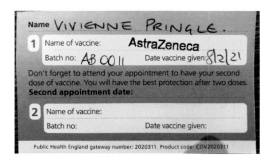
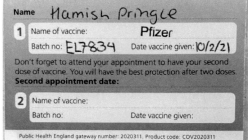

Covid-19: A child's view

HOW DID YOU FEEL BEING OFF SCHOOL?

Hattie, 8   I was sad because I couldn't see my friends.

Really happy beaca because you can get your work done really fast but really sad because I couldn't see my friends   Poppy, 8

Sad and lonely   Isobella, 8   sad and bored   Hugo, 9

Cassidy's coronavirus memory

Covid-19 is a horrible virus. Some people have got it, so that is why we have to wash our hands, wear a mask and make space. Covid-19 makes me feel worried because it makes me wonder what is going to happen next. I went to school and I had to sit in the next classroom. On the news all the Covid-19 things are happening.

Covid Drawing by Cassidy - aged 6

Nineteen

What is the term for a person or event who/which transmits an infectious disease to an unusually large number of people?

Questions

(ANSWERS IN BACK OF BOOK)

Covid A-Z

A - Anti-vaxxers/AstraZeneca/Antibacterial gel/Antibodies/Asymptomatic

B - Boris/Bubble

C - Coronavirus/Covidiots/Captain Tom/Contact tracing/Curfews/Continuous cough/Circuit breaker/Contagious/Conspiracy theories

D - Doorstep clapping for carers/Drive-through testing/Disinfecting surfaces/Daily exercise

E - Elbow sneezing/Essential outing/Eat out to help out

F - Face covering/ Furlough/Fundraising/Fever

G - Government guidelines/Government warnings/Gloves

H - Home deliveries/Hand sanitizers/Herd immunity/Home schooling/Hands-Face-Space/Hotel quarantine

I - Isolation/ICU overload/Immunity/Incubation period/Indoors

J - Job losses/Jabs

K - Key workers/Keep your distance/Kits (for testing)

L - Long Covid/Local lockdown/Lateral flow test

M - Masks/Mental health issues/Mutations

N - Nightingale hospitals/New normal/NHS heroes/News conferences

O - Online shopping/Online learning/Outbreak/Oxford vaccine

P - PPE/Pandemic/Pfizer

Q - Quarantine

R - Rioting/Rona/Respirator/Rule of six/R number/Recovery/ Roadmap(to recovery)

S - Stay at Home,Stay safe/Super spreader/Social distancing/Self isolating/Shielding/Stop the spread/Symptoms/Swab test/Scientific advice/Strains

T - Toilet roll hoarding/Tiers/Track and trace/Two metre distance/ Testing/Transmission

U - Unnecessary travel/Unprecedented times/Underlying conditions

V - Vaccine/Volunteering/Variants/Vulnerable/Ventilator/Visor/ Virtual meetings

W - Walking/WFH-Working from home/Washing hands/Wuhan

X - Virtual kisses

Y - Yoga online/Yesterday's clothes

Z - Zoom calls

Nineteen

10

Questions

What is the name of a method used to locate people who have been exposed to a confirmed case of an infectious disease?

(ANSWERS IN BACK OF BOOK)

A walk on the wild side

It's not every day that you turn 70, so I decided I wanted to do something special for my birthday. Instead of having cake with friends, I decided to walk 70 miles of the Wales Coast Path and raise money for Bournemouth Samaritans.

Lockdown gave me a perfect opportunity to train for it: I had time to spare and I wasn't able to go to my exercise classes or swimming. My daughter Jenny decided to join me, so we started preparing for the big event. We took long walks together and separately. I could do with the practice, because I had never done long walks on consecutive days. It's easier to exercise a lot one day, then take it easy the next... This was going to be a challenge.

We decided to walk to Swanage one day, stay in a friend's caravan overnight and then walk back the next day. The fact that I carried all my overnight stuff in a backpack was another first for me, so it all seemed good training. But it went well, and my confidence grew. Our Wales walk was planned for May, to coincide with my birthday, and I booked all the accommodation ahead. Then came the Covid restrictions and everything had to be cancelled. Things changed again, and I was able to rebook.

Sue

My father had lived near Harlech, his mother's family home, and I wanted to finish my walk there. We planned to walk for five days and the distances varied from 9 miles a day to 16.5 miles a day, depending on the accommodation. Our route went from Aberystwyth to Harlech.

Jenny and Sue

I had never walked for five solid days before, carrying a heavy rucksack with everything I needed, but it went better than I could have imagined.

The fact that I had run marathons certainly helped. What also helped was the weather. Another thing: the B&Bs we stayed in were perfect and the scenery was absolutely stunning. We walked along river valleys, through fields, up and down hills and, of course, along the coast. We both loved every minute of it.

And then there was the extra bonus: we had raised about £4000 for Bournemouth Samaritans. I have been overwhelmed by all the support and generosity of so many friends and acquaintances. But it will be a challenge to plan something special when I turn 80!

Sue Tipping

Waking up

This is how I recommend to start each day. It is, of course, the confirmation that we have made it to another day on precious Earth. There is the other sort of wake up which happens when you are so caught in a moment and you suddenly feel truly awakened to the beauty, serenity or reality of that moment.

My wake up, in the past, was often a little ritual I had to run though. Firstly, was I in the room alone? Was David with me? I would listen for his breath or stretch out an arm or leg to feel if it would reach the other side of the bed. With this information established, the opening of the eyes, Where am I today? After 27 years of flying for British Airways, mostly long haul, this is something I could never take for granted. A scan of the room for tell-tale signs. Could I recognise a hotel chain sign on the desk for wifi, or would it be the ornate cornice of an Indian hotel. The hotels in India, some of the most luxurious we stayed in, had a distinct aroma, of flowers, incense, spice and, almost earth.

David and Kevin

The world used to feel very small to me, after all I would go to work to do my job and step off in another continent. A quick flight to New York or Hong Kong felt like going home to me and required little more thought in my mind than planning a shopping trip to Salisbury nowadays.

I was lucky enough to have my partner, David, with me too most of the time because we flew together. David was the perfect travelling companion as he would quickly find out all that was going on in every destination and often procure great tickets to see things. I remember seeing Barry Manilow perform live under the Hollywood sign and feeling like he was singing just to me.

Then along comes Covid - creeping at first! Nobody really sure what it really meant for the World. How would it compare to all the pandemics that had come before. I remember we were due to fly to San Paulo - Brazil and we both said - let's pack a few more things in case work plans change and we get delayed in Brazil.

By the time we got to Brazil, the world was starting to change in an unprecedented way. Italy, Spain and Korea all reporting this virus was getting out of control. Then America announced that it was closing its air borders. The crew all met in the coffee shop - Brazil has great coffee and amazing cakes. Having gone through the Gulf War, 9-11, terrorism and volcanic ash we were all good at visualising the media frenzy about to ensue.

Waking up in Brazil on the last day I was filled with a mixture of anxieties. Was my aircraft en route? Would we take off? Would we get home? Were our travel plans on track and would David be with me? I remember the beautiful restaurant we had eaten in last night, the music, the warm air and yet, we were aware of a change that we couldn't quite put a finger on. I said to David, that this might be the last time we come here.

As we boarded the flight we were told of a delay as we had to take passengers from another flight from Chile. They had been denied board by two different cruise lines as the ships were not allowed to dock and these passengers had been told to go straight home as the world was starting to close down. I gave them champagne to ease their disappointment, and we made sure we made a fuss of them.

What more could we do! The flight was different, fear, kindness and rudeness and face masks everywhere. As crew, we were used to seeing face masks on Asian flights. Well now Europeans were wearing them too!

As we landed in London, a bumpy one, my fellow crew member said with a tear rolling down her cheek "I have a feeling this is my last landing with BA". I thought she was being over-dramatic. Little did I know what lay ahead.

Waking up this year has been a little different. I still wonder if David is beside me or if I'm in the guest room, being men of a certain age, we snore! During the last year our stress and anxiety grew to levels never experienced before. I seem to wake up at 2.30 most nights, often with a racing mind. It is, however, quite easy to work out where I am when I wake up, this last year it is always at home.

This year, like many other people, there have been no holidays as one by one they were cancelled. I feel caged at times; I have never spent so long in one place. My world feels the size of a postage stamp to me, or as I call it now, the world I can walk to from my front door. This new small world both bothers me and gives me comfort. I feel the loss of my big wide world.

We feel truly lucky to have seen so much of the world over the last 27 years. Sadly, we have experienced first-hand, the horrendous globalisation of our planet, then the internet, false news, extreme views. Don't get me wrong, I don't wish to send a letter strapped to an owl, there have been some amazing advantages. However, we are living with the detrimental effects of globalisation now. I will stop, as I'm beginning to feel a bit like Victor Meldrew having a middle-aged rant!

During my small life in 2020, I have learned much about myself and my friends. We miss company. We always knew we had an amazing set of friends but we've learned to be more selective. The effort some friends put in for you is so heart warming and a pleasure to return. I have learned the difference between a friend and an acquaintance. An acquaintance is a wonderful thing, bringing new life and freshness into yours. An acquaintance can light up your life for a few minutes and then be gone.

As we hit summer British Airways ramped up its desire to rid itself of as many staff as possible, particularly the older staff on more expensive contracts. Twelve thousand of us were to go. We had been so proud to wear our uniform and serve for this iconic British institution. Flying had been our way of life as well as our job. For both of us, our incomes were now under threat.

Wake ups in the night were frequent, alcohol in any quantity did not help. We were both trying to cope with the loss of our livelihood and our way of life. Things got dark. There were weeks when we could not help each other, I felt useless, old, unable to deal with what lay ahead. It felt like a bereavement - a living loss of the life I had had, and not on my terms. Two of our colleagues committed suicide, the pressure was huge.

We had to regroup, but how to portray yourself on a CV when you felt useless, when you had been thrown on the scrap heap. My dyslexia doesn't help, especially when I'm under pressure.

People told us "you'll be fine" and we are. But David and I went through a grieving process, often out of pace with each other.

David and I now work for a holiday home letting company and we love it. We can still work together and we are good at it. Through this company believing in us, we have both got our confidence and pride back. I think pride is very underrated, for me, finding it again has meant everything. We have had to re-jig our finances so we can still enjoy the things that are important to us. I love our home, castle, sanctuary and good food and entertaining friends with a meal when we have had snippets of greater freedom between lockdowns. They have been our priority for some time now.

As the anxiety and stress slowly subsided through Autumn and Christmas we had many wake up moments, the light on the sea, dogs playing on the beach, enjoying a coffee with a friend. We have found so much pleasure in being in the moment. Thankfully Covid has taught me take the time to enjoy all the small things.

Waking up in 2021 has a lovely sense of hope about it too. Sure I still check where I am in the morning, but hope and optimism help my feet to touch the floor. David and I have volunteered for marshalling duties at the Covid vaccination centre. We even had the vaccine ourselves to protect us while we are helping others over the next few months. Every person I see coming through the door is a step closer to getting through this pandemic. I have heard stories from people who haven't left their home for a year or who haven't spoken to another person for a week. I actually had a tear in my eye when I was vaccinated; the sense of hope for a brighter future came over me like a wave. I can see it in others too as they pass through. The NHS staff I work with are so positive, they have told me some of the things they have endured this last year. It makes your eyes water - but that's their story to tell.

So, as I draw to a close, I have big plans for the next chapter in my life. I will take some of the lessons learned from this Covid pandemic with me. In particular, I need less stuff! Be in the moment now. Treasure and look after a friend. You can only be responsible for you. Laughter is magic.

Thanks for your time.

Kevin and David volunteering at a vaccine centre

The bubble

Within the safety of a bubble, I discover my lock down lover
A connection from the age of four
Which passed us by, a sliding door
We walk, we talk, we share, we care
Rediscovering the connection, always there
Behind the mask within the bubble, we are safe
No eyes can see us in this place

Our bubble bursts as lockdown lifts
We lose our grasp on this precious gift
As life returns to a normal pace
We lose the safety of our place
Behind the mask is full of fear
Shadows of divorce come clear
Romance in the eye of a storm
Without chaos would not be born
A love that wasn't meant to last
Reminds me that "this too shall pass"

How quickly life hurries by, still no tears do I cry
Just gratitude for the chance
To embrace the beauty of a lockdown dance
To laugh, to love, to twist, to turn
An experience to grow and learn
Amidst the pain left by the rift, I remember the pleasure of my
lockdown gift

Nineteen

11

Questions

What is the practice of remaining at least two metres apart from others, when moving around in public areas?

(ANSWERS IN BACK OF BOOK)

Pantomime finale

Covid: the finale to a terrible film

My life prior to the lockdown was already like a really bad tragic film script. There were far too many backstories, in an already overstretched drama.

Where to start?

I suppose with the death of my husband, five days before the PM finally locked us down and gave us clarity on just how restricted we were to be.

Standing in a room by his coffin with my two grown up children, his sister and her husband. Socially distanced. No celebrant. No words spoken. What was the point? He was so loved and admired, Covid robbed him of the 400 or so people we knew would have said goodbye. A 10-minute farcical farewell to my darling husband after many years of stoically coping with procedure after procedure to help him breathe and not choke on his own saliva following throat cancer and catastrophic radiotherapy damage.

Not left to die alone

During his last four months I nursed Tim at home, as a silent aspiration left him doubly incontinent, unable to walk or speak. After a month in hospital, they wanted Tim to go to a nursing home, as his needs were so high, with his tracheostomy. The agency nurses equipped to deal with him were few and far between and very expensive. The battle I had to bring him home and fight for support was almost more than I could bear, after so many battles over the years. He had never given up sailing and just six months before had crewed with his friends for the Isle of Wight Round The Island race. He was 68 years old (14 years older than me) and was not going to be taken away from me and the children to die alone.

After a crash course in administering his night care in hospital, mastering the two-hourly nebulisers and suction to stop him choking, he came home. I will spare you the details of the toll this took. Tim's death was when I was supposed to finally let go of so much suppressed grief. In the year leading up to it my brother was found dead from an accidental overdose, my daughter was in a secretive, controlling relationship, my father who had Alzheimer's died - my sister and I spent a week in and out of hospital waiting for him to die after fluids were withheld. My mother had Alzheimer's and needed daily care from us both. My dog of 15 years then died. Too many backstories... In the meantime my husband's business went into administration and I struggled to keep my small cookery school going, as it was to be our only source of income. I am tempted to leave out that just before my husband died, we were victims of a scam and money was taken that was owed to my husband. It was never recovered. The day after my husband died my son was threatened about the legal action we were going to take. We withdrew. We were too shocked, devastated, numb. We had had enough.

Tim

Staying strong

I was never able to grieve. I had to hang on: I couldn't abandon my husband, kids and leave my parents solely for my wonderful, forever giving sister to care for. I had to learn to be strong once again when my son became depressed after his father's death. The lockdown was such terrible timing. He needed his friends. He didn't live with me and neither did my daughter. They had to grieve in their own way.

It was bittersweet though, not having to face people. I did what I always do and kept myself crazy busy. Like many people, I found the joy of gardening. My garden is now quite lovely after I spent hours and hours digging, thinking about my husband. I also discovered podcasts. They saved me Adam Buxton, Louis Theroux, Fortunately, Older and Wider. Mainly things that have made me laugh through my tears. I am lucky that I have always been self reliant, I think I was luckier than many in that respect.

Overnight I had no income.

My husband's disability and state pension ceased and even after giving myself some breathing space I could not run my cookery classes. I was lucky enough to receive the self-employment help from the government and for that I am hugely grateful. It has taken away the stress of having to worry about paying the bills.

Back into the world

So now we are coming out of this weirdest of years. There is a timeline for the rituals of grief for a reason and in many ways I am dreading the idea of seeing the many, many people Tim knew. I'm not sure the tears will stop for a while.

I am proud of myself though for getting through all of this. I have done my best. I discovered the joy of gardening and cycling, I bought a paddle board and invested in friendships I might otherwise have not. I have questioned relationships that don't make me happy and considering all, my contribution to the bottle bank has been fairly modest. God bless my beautiful husband and my wonderful children.

Preferential treatment

I am a 33 year-old bodyguard and personal trainer. On 30 September 2020, when around a quarter of the UK was entering a period of local lockdown due to the increase in Covid cases, I was the opposite of limited in my freedom: I was preparing to leave the country. I had been asked to travel to Pakistan as the bodyguard of a celebrity and his wife, and long before I left, I already discovered that things are a lot easier for some people than for others.

Before I could leave the country, I had to get a visa for Pakistan. It was the first indication that being famous, or associated with someone famous, can smooth your path, even when it comes to official paperwork. I had expected to wait for six to eight weeks for my visa, like everyone else, but mine arrived in three days.

We flew to Islamabad. I had never been to Pakistan before, and wondered what to expect, and even felt a bit apprehensive about the impact of Covid in such a densely populated country. However, as soon as we touched down, we were protected all the way. There is something called Protocol: police protection provided by the government 24 hours a day to important persons and their entourage. The protected person is called the Principal, and they certainly take their protection seriously in Pakistan. During the 10-day trip, we travelled everywhere in two cars, with one police escort car in front of us and one behind. It meant that we had a minimum of contact with the outside world, which was a great advantage in Covid time, and I felt safe and thankful.

The Principal was returning to Pakistan to host his first public event, to the great excitement of everybody involved. We received five star treatment everywhere we went, and I had the chance to meet several members of the government and dignitaries during the trip. There were photo shoots, appearances in the media... It was quite a wonderful experience. We did stick to Covid regulations and wore masks, but we felt well protected and seemed to live in a bubble of our own.

On our return we flew to Dubai for two nights and again, I noticed how differently our group was treated to other people. The rest of the passengers had to go through a whole series of procedures before they were allowed to enter the country. We, however, stepped off the plane and straight into two private cars. I have travelled a great deal in my lifetime, but this trip was a revelation. In a time where so many precautions were in place to protect travellers, we walked through the airport with no delay whatsoever. They say death is the great leveller, and I hope my Principal, a kind and courteous man, will never find out.

But even in Covid times, it seems that there is an other half, or maybe an other 5 percent, who live differently.

Alfie's lockdown experience

(Baden-Powell and St Peter's Church of England Junior School)

Over lockdown many challenges appeared like home schooling and lots of shops closed. My mum is a teacher, one of the key-workers. On the first lockdown I was home schooled. Personally, I thought home schooling would be amazing but how wrong I was (my brother was being home schooled as well.) My dad was always in the office it was terrible. There was always unfinished work- there was all ways so much stress. My mum was always on the computer helping the children in her class. Before lockdown, when we went to the shop, I would look around and see people shouting "get your fruit here as fresh as it could be," but now I look around all I see is closed shops and massive queues. When you get into the shop, you see people with masks on. Arrows on the floor; one way system stay two metres apart from each other! More people are ordering online and people are getting lazy. This is something I have not mentioned yet but is very shocking; people have been taken by this monstrosity called covid-19.

Some of my family members have been taken as well. Teachers have been amazing it is sad to think that some teachers don't get the respect that they deserve; it has taken all of this for some teachers to get the respect that they deserve and some teachers still don't get respect. In the second lockdown many things were different. I was at school and so was my brother but not all my friends were there and I started to miss them. My grandma passed away and she lives about three hours away and my nan lives about two hours away so I had to take time off school to go to the funeral.

Over all, lockdown was rubbish but something I reminded myself is when a storm comes along, no matter how long, blue skies always follow.

By Alfie - Year 6

In dedication

A truly awesome thing you have done. On behalf of Fred's love of the RNLI please accept this small contribution to your wonderful creation!

John Powell

Alex W's lockdown experience

(Baden-Powell and St Peter's Church of England Junior School)

For me, it has been a really hard lockdown. The challenges I have been through were really hard and I just wanted to give up – but I didn't. I chose my path and I got to the end of it and then, I realised that it wouldn't stop me from doing anything.

My story for lockdown was life-changing. I could only be with a few people: My parents, my friends and myself. But my parents are the ones I most admired in lockdown because they were key workers. Since they were key workers I could still go to school but with a twist, I could not touch, or hug, or even a high-five but I still had a lot of fun. When we aren't in lockdown, we go to school. But with lockdown it was different- a lot different. Some people had to do home learning and others can go to school, if their parents are key workers. Some people feel a bit sad because they don't get to see anybody except your family.

Fortunately, on the 8th of March, people can meet together and have a great time.

To conclude, it's alright now because I know that I can keep away from Covid-19 by washing your hands regularly, staying at home and saving lives.

I hope you do too.

By Alex W - Year 6

Nineteen

12

What is the practice of staying at home and not mixing with others for a period of time, to avoid the spread of a disease?

Questions

(ANSWERS IN BACK OF BOOK)

Louise C's lockdown experience

(Baden-Powell and St Peter's Church of England Junior School)

Lockdown has been tough for all of us and lots of us have had to lose loved ones. I thankfully haven't lost someone yet but I sympathise for those who have.

During lockdown I have become closer to my family and play with my sisters more often. One of the hardest struggles for me during lockdown was that I couldn't see my friends and family. I missed them so much and it was hard for me to cope sometimes. Another thing that affected me a bit was growing up and my hormones as I sometimes would get annoyed and angry at someone or something for no reason. I put my hands down to all of those key-workers such as hospital workers, teachers and lots more. I admire all of the work that they do.

My mum works in the hospital as a diabetes nurse and works so so hard and sometimes she got home so late that me and my sisters were either in bed, asleep or it was like 21:00. I also missed swimming and being in the water. Thankfully, we have the beach and I loved going there but it would have been a lot better if I were with my friends.

To conclude this, if we can all get through this and stay safe we can get through anything if we are all together.

By Louise C - Year 6

Nineteen

13 What is the name of a method of controlling a disease using isolation?

Questions

(ANSWERS IN BACK OF BOOK)

Jude S's lockdown experience

(Baden-Powell and St Peter's Church of England Junior School)

Generally, lockdown has made me think about the small things, like the wonderful places I can go, just right outside my doorstep. The beautiful views near my house and the seaside. For me, the beach was mostly open, which meant we really appreciated it.

Before lockdown hit, me and my family used to visit the beach a lot and owned are own beach hut. We would go down to the seaside and play in the sand, splash in the sea and watch the sun in the distance. As much as we enjoyed it, I think we really took it for granted. Some people have to travel along way just to enjoy the waves. When lockdown came, thousands of people stormed the beaches for their exercise and we couldn't go because of the Covid rules. So, after that we really appreciated where we lived a lot more. I think a lot of other people did too as when we go for a beach walk down by the waves, I notice a lot more people enjoying the beaches with us. That was something that kept me from going insane in lockdown. And that is a good thing in itself.

So, if you take anything from this, if you appreciate what you have, life will become a lot better and you will get through lock down a lot quicker.

By Jude S - Year 6

In dedication

To all those who have lost loved ones.
To all those who have lost their lives.
To all those who have survived this terrible virus.

WPG

Jude W's lockdown experience

(Baden-Powell and St Peter's Church of England Junior School)

For me, life in lockdown has been emotional, not being able to go to friends' houses, and birthdays not being as enjoyable, without many people around. It has also been challenging, testing my patience and my durability.

Yet every cloud has a silver lining, and this is mine: there are a few people that prefer in to out, and I am one of those people. Having to stay indoors, I have had more time for activities that I enjoy, such as reading, playing **indoor** games, and of course, using my hyperactive imagination, whilst pacing up and down my room.

sigh If I could describe lockdown in three words those three words would be: **very very annoying.**

By Jude W - Year 6

Covid-19: A child's view

WHAT IS YOUR WORST MEMORY OF LOCKDOWN?

when my dad got covid-19 and my family had to self isolate on Christmas.
Alexandra, 8

going off school
Luke, 8

Arguing about masks
Harriet, 8

lots of fall outs because of not being able to go out.
Poppy, 8

My nan braking her sholder
Isaac, 8

Barry's birthday

My birthday is on the 16th April, and on that date in 2020 we were a month into lockdown. There were no bubbles with other parts of families. Our daughter, son in law and three grand-daughters lived only 5 miles away but could only meet in a socially distanced way.

Normally we would be celebrating my birthday with them with a good meal but no chance this year. However one of my grand-daughters baked a small birthday cake, complete with candles, and brought it over.

Barry and his birthday cake

We had set up a table on the drive and the cake was placed on it a safe distance away from the gate. The weather was happily fine and this photo is of me cutting the cake with a family looking on leaning on the gate.

It was the closest we could get to a family occasion – but it gave us a chance to have a much-needed laugh !

Covid – life revised

The Story of Sheryl and Phil

Life can change so suddenly. We have always been keen travellers, experiencing different cultures, meeting people, listening to new music and – of course – tasting different foods. We often used to say that we travel to eat... We have had the most wonderful memories of foreign countries, and for 2020, we had a number of trips planned as well. Life seemed good.

And then suddenly, there was COVID. No more travelling, no more trips. We lost money on cancellations, but flying was out of the question. Safety was far more important. When you're faced with a pandemic, your priorities change. Drastically, even.

We live in a small town, Wading River, on eastern Long Island, New York, and now that there are no flights to take, holidays to book or travel preparations to make, we have discovered a whole new world to travel in: our own neighbourhood. Right on our doorstep, there are beautiful deer, birds, squirrels, chipmunks, and many varieties of large trees. I've seen sights I've never noticed before: fawns suckling and deer standing on their hind legs to eat out of our bird feeder. There is a beach nearby, where we can walk or cycle, and all summer and autumn long, we have swum and kayaked in nearby Long Island Sound or in the ocean. Several times a week we put our bikes on the car and ventured out to quiet side streets, or to Peconic Bay, where we found hidden beaches that we had all to ourselves. Adventure can be found close to home, it seems.

We also discovered that you don't have to fly to another country to taste new food. We tried new, exciting recipes, sourcing the produce on our local farms. And when we had overindulged in the local cheeses and irresistible chocolate, we did yoga, Tai Chi and Zumba with our neighbours. When winter came, we wrapped up warm and still went on bike rides – except in January, when a snowstorm kept us inside for a week. At 73 and 74, we found a whole new way of life.

There is sadness, of course. We hardly ever see our grandchildren, who live one hour away from us. We exchanged Christmas presents outside, under a heat lamp, and it was heart breaking not to be able to hug them. Thank heaven for FaceTime. We miss going out and seeing friends, but there, too, FaceTime helps. We know we are lucky: we have each other for company and if we need a bit of 'spousal distancing', we sit in separate rooms and meet up later to watch a film together.

It's been almost a year now that we have been living in this crazy, strange world. But it's not all bad, in spite of the fear and the tragedies. We have just celebrated President Biden's inauguration, and are looking forward to a welcome change. It's been a brutal past four years and hopefully America can come together peacefully now. We are also proud to have a strong woman Vice President. The Biden/Harris team has a challenging road ahead and we wish them the best. We have had our first vaccination, and look forward to – very cautiously - returning to our normal life once we get the final vaccine. But if there is one thing we have learned over the past year it is this: we will never take the 'normal' things in life for granted again.

The worst Christmas present

Christmas Day, 2020

Work had been more hectic than ever in the weeks before Christmas this Covid year. I was so glad that restrictions allowed three households to mix: my parents, my uncle and I had planned to have Christmas at my house and I was really looking forward to the break. We didn't know then that we were going to get the one present that nobody wanted for Christmas...

On Boxing Day we met my brothers and family outdoors. My uncle looked pale and left early. On Sunday 27th, my uncle was sick, with an upset stomach, but we were all fine, so my mum and dad came for dinner. The next evening, I developed a sore throat, and the day after that I had a cold. My mum and dad would soon follow...

On Monday evening I felt that the cold was progressing, so I had a hot bath and put on new PJs. The fire was lit, the tree lights on, I had a couple of glasses of wine and my little dog fell asleep on me. I decided to return to my childhood and sleep on the sofa watching Bridgerton.

The next morning I awoke full of cold, with pressure in my sinuses, a headache, a sore throat, a runny nose and feeling chilly. I also had a very stiff neck and shoulders, which I thought was due to sleeping on the sofa. When I got into the shower the water hurt my scalp and skin. Still feeling cold I wrapped up, lit the fire again and decided to watch TV all day. I called my parents to see how they were feeling and they told me they were fine. As the day progressed I was getting a little worried as my temperature seemed to be fluctuating from 34 degrees to 37 degrees, but I convinced myself that I was getting paranoid and all I had was a cold.

On Wednesday, after a good night's sleep thanks to Night Nurse and wine, I awoke feeling pretty much the same. The headache was still present, my temperature was normal by now, my neck, shoulders and upper back were still stiff, but apart from being cold I felt okay. Later that day, I attended a funeral and that was when I realised how much I was trying to stifle a cough. After the funeral, when I was walking my dog in the woods, I got a phone call from my brother who had popped by my parents to say hello through the window. He told me they both looked terrible, and had a persistent cough and cold symptoms. He had ordered a Covid test for them, to be delivered at their home, and I decided to book myself one. I was about to phone work to let them know that I would not be in the following day, when they called me to inform me that we were going into lockdown again.

On 31st December I had a Covid test at Southampton Airport. As you are told to behave as if you have Covid-19 until you receive your negative results, I stayed at home all day, but by now I was actually feeling better and quite confident the test would be negative. Happy New Year!!!

Not so Happy New Year

On January 1st I still had cold symptoms. I could not get warm, my feet were freezing, I even looked online to buy some Uggs! No test results yet. The next day I still was cold, but definitely feeling better. I was keen to get the results so that I could go out to walk the dog and go grocery shopping. Later that evening I decided to spend the evening cooking, something I love to do but it was the first time that I had really wanted to since having my parents for dinner that Sunday. I cracked open a bottle of Sauvignon Blanc and got cooking, enjoying the wine and Liza Tarbuck's company on Radio 2. I even ventured into the garden for the first time since Sunday, for a rare cigarette. Back in the kitchen I started making a pasta sauce from scratch, and got a call from a friend for a quick catch-up. Then I noticed the text: NHS POSITIVE! I couldn't believe it. I called my parents to tell them the news. They still had not received their results but I was pretty sure they would be positive too as our symptoms were exactly the same. My uncle had, by now, found out that he too had Covid.

That Sunday, I could hardly believe I was positive. I was still cold all the time and had a runny nose, but that was it. I was more concerned about my parents because they felt terrible. The news footage of hospitals being overrun, people on ventilators, more and more positive test results and an increasing amount of people dying within twenty-eight days of a positive test just sent my anxiety levels through the roof: how ill were we going to get? The worst scenarios were playing in my head: what if my parents were hospitalised and we wouldn't be able to see them or - God forbid - be with them when they needed us most? The following day their results came back positive; no surprise there. However, they both were beginning to feel a little better. The relief was incredible.

That evening I poured myself a glass of wine. I took one sip and it was like drinking paint stripper (not that I have ever done that). I sprayed myself with a very strong fragrance and couldn't smell a thing. It then occurred to me that I hadn't eaten much at all and what I had eaten, I hadn't really liked. This, of course, is another symptom. After three or four days both senses started to return. Wine still tasted awful but I could definitely taste gin and strong flavoured food, thank God. By now both parents were feeling better. They seemed to have taken longer to recover, which I believe was to be expected.

The lucky ones

I wanted to share my story as I think it is important to know that for some of us who have survived Covid - the lucky ones - it wasn't as severe as it has been for others.

Seven weeks down the line and I am happy to say we have all fully recovered. You start to feel better as time goes by, then one day you wake up and think: 'Wow yes, I feel like me again!' And great news: I can definitely taste wine again.

Covid–19: A child's view

WHAT IS YOUR FAVOURITE MEMORY OF LOCKDOWN?

going to the fish shop with my nanny
Alice, 8

geting a pet
Rosie, 8

walking my dog poppy.
Jonah, 8

playing football in my garden
Victor, 7

Artwork by Luke Gevell

In dedication

Yassamin is an inspirational Pilates instructor who is very highly qualified and passionate about her work. She is constantly learning and evolving in her teaching so all her clients benefit. Thank you so much for enabling us to live a pain free life – which is priceless!

We feel so privileged to know Yassamin, she is such a sensitive and lovely person, we really admire her kindness and compassion to others. She has also worked very hard and dedicated so much time and energy into getting this wonderful book published in aid of Charity. She is simply amazing!

Cheryl and Dave Ashton

If this time

If this time has taught me anything, it is that the tiny spec in this universe that we occupy, is both wonderful and wondrous, and if we allow it to, the beauty around us, can unlock the beauty within us; and teach us far more than our schooling ever did.

If this time has taught me anything, it is that success, and how we measure it, needs to be re-defined, and that the only person to whom you should ever compare yourself, is who you were yesterday. Make your growth-game strong, and along the way, be kind to yourself - if you are doing your best, you are doing enough.

If this time has taught me anything, it is that it is more important now than ever before, to see the world through your own eyes. Begin by looking at yourself - look honestly and gently. Look inward with compassion and kindness, and look outward with humility and appreciation.

If this time has taught me anything, it is that the opposite of love is not hate, but fear – and our greatest fear is losing that to which we have become attached. Yesterday is heavy, put it down. Seeing the beauty in the world around you is the first step in purifying and clearing the mind, and if this time has taught me anything, it is that nature, unlike us, never apologises for her beauty.

If this time has taught me anything, it is that life really is about the journey, not the destination - and it must be, for surely we are not here merely to reach the destination, for the destination is death. Be alive, for after all, life is all you've got, and when you pay attention to the things for which you are grateful, you soon forget about what you think you're missing.

If this time has taught me anything, it is that bitter tears are the quietest, and on the days when your head wants to hang low, it is important that you look up. Lift your head. Take it in, and breathe deep, for while this world can sometimes be a hard place, your reality and what you perceive it to be, are seldom aligned.

If this time has taught me anything, it is that beauty truly is in the eye of the beholder. We can see universes, within universes - but only when we pay enough attention, and this is as true of the nature within us, as it is of the nature around us.

If this time has taught me anything, it is this: If true love conquers everything, then self-love gives it the fortitude to do so. Know that you are more than your scars – know that every wound in you that has healed along the way has taught you what it is to fight back; and to start again from where you are, with what you've got, without seeking the approval of others and know that self-love is not vanity.

If this time has taught me anything it is this: HOPE matters, and we cannot live without it. This time has taught me that HOPE is not a wish, nor a desire for things to be different. It is a course of action, a combination of mind and heart. The future can be better and can be brighter, and we each have the power within us to make it so.   There will be challenges to face along the way, to which there are many solutions. There is a source of resilience deep within us all.

If this time does not teach us that time itself is precious, then we will have missed the lesson. The lesson that never before have the past and the future been so irrelevant, and that the quest to 'find ourselves' has been fruitless to now; only because we've been searching in all the wrong places.

We are here, we are now. We are each and every breath we take. Every day is a gift – a gift to begin again, and to grasp with both hands, the fresh opportunity to learn, unlearn and re-learn. If this time...........is not wasted.

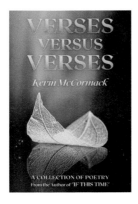

Poem included with the
kind permission of
Kevin McCormack
from his poetry collection
Verses Versus Verses.

The real face of Covid

Anneke's story

Covid crept into our lives at the end of December 2020. My husband and I had a cough and felt tired, so the GP sent us for tests and they came back positive. Two weeks in isolation, with symptoms that were rather mild seemed quite doable. And it stayed like that for my husband, but my health deteriorated drastically. On January 5th I was taken to hospital by ambulance, and from then on everything is a blank. I was put into an induced coma straight away. They kept me in a coma for four weeks; I was on a respirator, ended up in intensive care for a week... all without me knowing about it. When I was finally woken up I was completely paralysed. All I could move was my fingers. I had no idea where I was; I thought I had been in an accident and it was absolutely terrifying. I was in a hospital room for two, which I found distressing, but they wouldn't move me to a single room until I was able to press the bell to ring a nurse. I can't tell you how many times I practiced that, ringing the bell, and in the end I managed and got a room of my own.

Anneke before Covid

I have no idea why Covid hit me so hard, and where I caught it. I had always been careful, not seen people, worn gloves to go shopping, put on a mask... In the early days in rehabilitation, I kept wondering and thinking about it, but the doctors said I mustn't dwell on it. It could have happened unpacking the shopping, forgetting to wash my hands, touching something with contaminated gloves, whatever... They wanted me to stop thinking about it, to stop wasting energy on negative things.

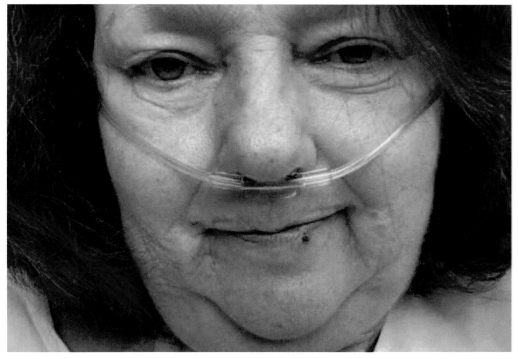

Anneke with Covid

One thing I do remember is having nightmares, which must have occurred while I was in a coma. I saw myself lying in a huge room, with lots of LED lights on the ceiling, and two nurses dressed in astronauts' suits, helmets and all, telling me I was not allowed to fall asleep, and shaking me. I talked about it with a psychologist, and they told me it could have to do with the fact that they turn you while you're in a coma, on your front, on your back... I might have felt that, I'll never know. But it's good to be able to talk about these experiences. I wouldn't wish on my worst enemy what I have been through. There are no words for it.

It is now the 17th of March and I am working hard to get stronger. I've slowly, slowly gained control over my body again. I can now walk up and down the hospital corridor with my Zimmer frame – as long as someone is with me - and today, for the first time, I have been on a treadmill. But my lung capacity is still only 50%, and I don't know if there will be permanent damage. I hope to get to 80%, and sometimes I feel deeply frustrated. It has been a long, hard struggle and there is still quite a way to go.

First, I was in a stage of denial, now I feel anger. I haven't been able to touch my husband's hand since that early January. He can come and see me, from a distance, but it's like having a gin & tonic put in front of you, and not being allowed to drink it. It's been hell for him, of course, and for my whole family. He's stayed in touch with the family via WhatsApp all the time I was in a coma, and now, at last, I can join them in the chats, and that helps. But I miss them all desperately, of course. He has taken pictures when I was in coma, but I'm not allowed to see those images until I'm completely better. And that's a while away.

It took me quite a bit of courage to show the picture of me in the hospital. But one evening, when I was watching the news on television, I saw nearly a thousand young people gathering in the street, partying, and it upset me deeply. I cried and cried, and I decided to take this selfie to show others what Covid can do to you. I shared the picture on Facebook, and got so many reactions, and personal messages, from people who were deeply shocked. Which is what it was all about. This is the face of Covid the world needs to see.

I will be in hospital for at least another month, maybe longer, until I can walk independently, and safely. There are times that I get discouraged, but the doctors say I have come a long way in a short time: from being completely paralysed to being able to go on a treadmill. Maybe I should write it all down, the progress I have made. Anyway, I'll stay as long as is needed. The bad thing is that there is Covid in the hospital, and the nurses and doctors come in in full PPE, which is frightening...
I do think that this experience has changed me. My husband and I have always lived life to the full, but I think we will do that even more now. We want to grab every opportunity, enjoy whatever we can, whenever we can. I feel as if I have been given a second chance. I am angry, I am sad, but I am here, in a bed with crisp white sheets, while I could have been in a coffin. Once you realise that, your life changes forever.

Lost and found

Love
Lost through the end of a 30 year marriage, found in the support and kindness of friends and family

Friendship
Lost by saying goodbye to those who will no longer be part of my life, found in rekindling old friendships and developing new

Happiness
Lost in a life wrapped in hope and effort, found through the little things, kind words, supportive gestures, bold actions

Hope
Lost in a future imagined, found in the glimmer of a different exciting expanse of opportunity

Future Dreams
Lost as the rug was pulled from under my feet, found through allowing myself to set free limitations and dare to imagine new possibilities

Freedom
Lost through pandemic restrictions, found through realising what is important and spending precious time with loved ones

Passion
Lost through missing safe companionable love, found in exciting new adventures with different people

Energy
Lost through grief and the need to keep going, found through the vitality and support of others

Simple Pleasures
Lost the experiences and simple joys I held dear, found through being reminded of what delights are around us every day

A poem from Canada

Covid for me has not been too bad,

Fortunately, I have not sat around and made myself sad,

I flew in from Shanghai on January 19th 2020

Spending a month in Asia was a glorious sanctuary, never empty,

Nothing was announced, so there life was all the same,

But when I came home to Vancouver, the mood had changed,

Clicking on CNN or BBC news, the pandemic was everywhere,

But nobody took it too seriously, not even America,

Canada started early with the masks and the cleaning of hands,

I could not sing happy birthday all day long, I count to 40 instead and then did a dance,

People were busy around the world, sending messages and videos of funny Covid clips,

I was too busy to read them until one day I sat on the couch and laughed and threw out my hips,

Videos came constantly; I longed to receive another as they cheered me up,

I would send them to my friends and family and thank goodness for whatsapp,

The world was making us laugh, creativity had surged, sharing began out of time and skill,

So out I went with my camera and verse, sending videos to Brits or Europeans was a thrill,

Fitness and exercise is my love, but I can hardly touch my toes,

Swinging my legs and arms around like a person picking their nose,

My legs are getting stiff as I sit all day at home. My fat thighs wobble as I stand and giggle

Not being able to move to straighten up, I hope I don't pee in my pants and do a piddle,

Hoping for this virus will finish, so I can go outside freely and be in my zone,

Vancouver has many spots I love to see, down by the river or walking through the trees,

The mountains call me and I get out my skis, living in Vancouver, Covid has not bothered me.

The stress is off, a few friends only to see, no planned dates or dinners or teas,

This gives me time to be by myself, only to fail at clearing my place for who? to come and see,

People are asked to stay at home, we are the good ones, but we hear we are not alone,

Off to the islands, the vineyards, the boats, they are not as careful as they venture the unknown,

Covid is a killer if you are old and grey, but outside is ok if you remember the drill,

Wear your mask, wash your hands, keep your distance and try and stay still on the hill,

Life is worth living, be creative and share, spend your time giving and you will find prayer,

Hop on your bike, put on your shoes, go for a walk and listen to the birds out there.

Music is a gift we all need to embrace, turn up the volume and let's raise our heads in grace.

Love yourself and find a close friend, a parent or a sibling, hopefully they will smile and relate.

The days are getting longer, the skies are opening up, if there is rain that's ok, we are tough,

Counting the hours before we go to bed, is this what happens when there's nothing else instead

We are the lucky ones, we have space out here, I still play tennis and a few friends I do see,

So get off the couch and walk along the street, we never know who you will see, it could be me!

Sue from Vancouver, Canada

A deserted Vancouver

The Marsh family

Fun, fundraising and friends all over the world

The last year has been a very strange one for us as a family, because although we have been cut off from people for long periods, we have also managed to make friends all over the world!

Music has always been a family hobby and from the time the children were very small, we have created songs and videos for family and friends. As the kids grew, so did their musical talent and skills, so when we went into lockdown last March, we decided to make a video of us doing a parody of a song from the musical Les Mis that Ben had changed the lyrics to. We practised for a couple of days and then recorded ourselves on a Sunday afternoon – arguments and all! Late on Sunday night we posted our 'One Day More' video on Ben's Facebook and tagged family and friends who were having birthdays we would miss. We woke the next morning to find the video had 'gone viral' and millions of people had viewed it. Over the next two weeks, we rode a rollercoaster of interviews and requests and received the most amazing messages from people who had suffered loss, and from people who had been working long shifts in hospitals or who were really struggling with being alone. It made us feel like we were making a difference while staying in our own house and we encouraged people to donate money to the WHO Covid-19 fund along with our own appearance fees.

We decided to set up our own YouTube channel and continued to put out songs based on our own frustrations or 'lockdown' experiences. We found it was a great way to do things together that didn't revolve around a screen! Then in January 2021 we recorded 'Have The New Jab', based on Leonard Cohen's 'Hallelujah', which was a song encouraging people to talk about any concerns they had about the vaccine. It was really popular with medics and was even shared by the UK's Chief Scientist, Sir Patrick Vallance. We felt the need to channel the positive reactions we got, so we started a fundraiser for Save the Children and raised £1,000. Then in February we recorded our take on Bonnie Tyler's 80s classic which we called 'Totally Fixed Where We Are'. Crazily enough, it went viral again! We were contacted by the people from Comic Relief and asked to perform on their live show, which we did on March 19th, still in our pyjamas! Our own fundraising,

The Marsh Family on Red Nose Day

which we boosted with ad revenue from another song we wrote called 'We're Not Singing Sea Shanties', made over £13,000 for Red Nose day.

Our videos have all had at least one mistake in them, but we try and show the reality of family life and the challenges of getting six people to all perform at the same time! Most of the songs are suggested by Ben and he begins to change the words, but we all offer our own ideas, and say what we like and what we don't! Some take a day or two to practise and record, but if they involve instruments, they can take a little longer. Our videos have been a great distraction for us and they also seem to have helped other people express their frustrations, recognise their own concerns or just laugh a little. The pandemic has been difficult for everyone, but we have felt an amazing connection with people around the world, and a shared desire for a better future. Which is something we've really cherished!

Much Love
The Marsh Family xx

The preserving jar

January 2020 was miserable: the UK was hit with one storm after another and in the background of our daily news there were vague reports of a virus on board cruise ships far, far away, and of people in Wuhan becoming unwell. And so it began.

In the care home I would always greet our residents with a wave, a smile, a hug or even a kiss on the hand, and we would chat about families and friends who had recently visited or upcoming family birthdays. The home was filled with chatter and laughter, entertainers came to amuse the residents and there was so much singing... Friends came for lunch or tea and our coffee shop was bustling with visitors enjoying drinks and homemade cake. But over the weeks and months, life started to change. THEN SILENCE.

Slowly, the roads become quiet, distances are kept - no visitors allowed. The coffee shop is a skeleton of its former self. But we are British, so we soldier on. We phone and Zoom or Face Time or whatever (but all Elsie wants is a hug from her daughter!). 'It will pass', we say. A new phase in the pandemic begins and visits are allowed behind screens (BUT NO TOUCHING). Hurrah and hurray, the residents can have visitors in their rooms, as long as they cover themselves from head to foot in plastic.

For some, this regime is an annoying inconvenience, for others it's just a joke, but to those who struggle with each waking moment it's like plunging down Alice in Wonderland's rabbit hole, without anything wonderful happening. Panic, anger, frustration and fear are vented in harsh words spoken to us, but we carry on regardless. Time ticks on and it's a new year. Optimism sprouts like new life in spring.

Then LOCKDOWN 3 begins. COVID has mutated – so now working has become ritualistic. Every day I ask myself if I have unsuspectingly become the grim reaper, carrying a deadly virus that could harm my colleagues, the residents, my family!

I wake, swab my throat and nose, wait for 30 minutes. It's like a pregnancy test in reverse – I DON'T WANT TO BE POSITIVE.

I go to work and smother myself in anti-bacterial gel, I wash my hands, change my clothes, cleanse the workstation. Beatrice comes over for a chat; I smile with my eyes because my mask covers my face. 'What's that you're saying?' she asks. 'I can't understand you, you're muffled.' We laugh.

A colleague passes. I ask: 'How's Cyril doing?' She turns, eyes like shiny puddles – he's gone, last Sunday. We fall silent, unable to offer comfort with a hug. Elbow bumps don't really have the same meaning at a time like this.

Routines are kept, entertainment is organised, Zoom calls are booked into diaries. The only visitors allowed are those who come every day, to spend time with their loved one and say goodbye. Death continues, COVID or not.

Lyn - Care Worker

The grand plan

My wife and I have always been involved in the hospitality industry, and since 2006 we have always lived in one of our hotels. However, there comes a time when you want a change, so after another hectic season in 2019, we decided it was time to sell up the place we had called home. In February 2020, one month before lockdown, we received an offer for the full asking price for the hotel. We were delighted! Finally, we could move in into a proper home and we would no longer be on call 24/7, waiting for the bell to tell us that guests wanted us.

During Covid I kept in touch with the buyer, who was keen to proceed. I helped him with projections and ideas, but we couldn't rest easy. We were dreading a phone call that said 'I can't proceed'. And sure enough it came, in mid-June, three weeks before the hotels could open again. We had to act quickly.

Plan B

I knew that Brexit had forced European workers to return to their own country and now Covid meant that many of them would not be returning to the UK. The hospitality industry cannot work without Eastern European employees. In other words: we were seriously short-staffed. I needed a plan B.

Because 33% of people who come to stay in Bournemouth are looking for room only, we decided to completely refurbish and re-brand the hotel and concentrate on income. We would employ a live-in manager and move from the hotel into an apartment. It was November 2020, and our savings from the summer season enabled us to push ahead with our plans. Winter is the quiet time in the hotel industry, so we took advantage of this time to get all the work completed. The hotel is now very contemporary and luxurious and guests come and stay on a room-only basis. So far, it looks as if it was absolutely the right move to make. We have also refurbished the two other hotels and I am happy to say they are all running very well.

Much to my wife's delight, we moved into a flat with beautiful sea views. We had forgotten what it was like to go home at night and we love it. We have found a suitable live-in manager and prepared ourselves for an easier life. During 2020, we constantly adjusted and fine-tuned our plans to ensure we were ready once the restrictions were eased. All in all, our Covid story seemed to be a fairly happy one.

And then...

We regard ourselves as reasonably sharp people, who know what is going on in the world. One of the things that is going on, is cyber crime. I have read many stories about it, and seen the documentaries on TV, and I was pretty sure I would know it if someone was trying to scam me. But of course there is always someone cleverer than you (if you can call scamming clever).

We were scammed for tens of thousands of pounds in a series of four emails, and when we look back, we can see that the way it was done, was so simple, but so clever. And all this at a time when we were running short of capital and relying on income to pay the final bills to our suppliers. We felt sick. It does not look like we will retrieve any of the money lost.

Stay alert!

So this was quite a happy Covid story until the very end, when it turned very sour. We are now struggling after all our refurbishment work and our plans for the business.

I understand that cyber crime is and continues to be at epidemic levels since lockdown began. So if nothing else, I hope that this will make all of you look very carefully at every transaction that is over £2000.00. And if you are paying a large amount of money, take a trip to the bank and get them to do it; that way if it all goes wrong you will be protected. Hopefully we will trade well this summer and pay off our debts..

Nineteen

14

What is the name of a group of people who remain together exclusively, in an effort to support each other, yet prevent further spreading of a disease?

Questions

(ANSWERS IN BACK OF BOOK)

Marina's reflection on a crisis

Hope springs eternal

I'm writing this on the anniversary of the first Covid 19 lockdown. That was the day everything stopped. The roads went quiet, the skies were quiet, the birds sang louder than ever and the dawn chorus was a cacophony of competitive birdsong. The sun shone, jokes were exchanged on social media. Zoom was no longer just a medium for virtual business meetings; it became a favourite way for families and friends to communicate or play quiz games. Shops closed, so did cinemas and theatres and cafes and restaurants and nobody went out. Children were home schooled as all the schools closed too. It felt like a holiday to me and to my daughter. My daughter is in her mid-thirties and a wheelchair user because of a degenerative condition.

Suddenly there was nothing that had to be done, nowhere we had to go. The sense of relief was enormous particularly for me because in the week prior to lockdown I had had Covid symptoms which made me very tired. I didn't realise it until my daughter's birthday, when I lost all senses of smell and taste completely. Because of lockdown my daughter's birthday meal, which should have been celebrated with her friends at our home, became a family affair with just my son, daughter and myself. They had to check the seasoning of the meal because I had no means of telling whether there was too much basil or salt or pepper or whether it was edible at all! That evening I was so exhausted that my daughter told me I looked as though I was dying.

The following day I heard that an ear, nose and throat consultant had reported a steep rise in patients complaining of loss of smell and taste, and he suggested that it might be Covid-linked. He was ignored by the UK government; the World Health Organisation hadn't listed it as a symptom. Two more months later, they did. But in the meantime I read that anecdotal evidence of this symptom had been noticed in South Korea, France and New York. I decided to consider myself as having Covid because my daughter's carers needed to know. They chose to remain away for the next fortnight to protect their other vulnerable clients.

It felt more like a holiday than ever: not only did we not have to go anywhere, we could get up when we liked, spend as much time as we wanted getting ready and eat breakfast at any time. We no longer had to take the timing of the carers, those valuable contributors to our lives, into account. This freedom from any timetable enhanced that holiday feeling. Somehow the restrictions mattered little at that time. One lovely carer did our food shopping and always bought some nice treats: chocolate bars, delicious salted caramel or chocolate biscuits, fresh blueberry muffins or doughnuts. In fact, by her third visit I found myself first checking the shopping bags for the treats, like an excited little child. Which bag had she put them in? Never mind the food!

We went out for afternoon walks, stopping to chat, at a social distance, with neighbours we hadn't seen through the winter. We joked about greeting with elbow bumps, not missing hugs… yet. We sat in the garden in the sunshine. In the afternoon, carers came to play board games with my daughter, or paint fingernails and toenails or try new plaited hairstyles. Every day I felt such a sense of relief that we have a lovely house and garden and beautiful surroundings in which to be restricted.

Bad news and moments of joy

Upsetting news came through, of overstretched hospitals, queuing ambulances, dedicated and overworked health professionals, a soaring infection rate, the horror of an increasing death rate and the grief of families who could not be with their dying relatives. We heard about people furloughed from their jobs, others with no jobs, an increase in the use of food banks, an increase in violence in the home. There was news about parents trying hard to keep up some sort of education for their children, with nowhere to go apart from the daily walk close to home.

One group benefited for a short time: homeless people were taken off the streets and housed in hotels. Apparently the government estimate of around 4,000 homeless was a highly conservative one. The number was closer to 43,000 and probably counting. We began to see that not only were many lives being lost; many were losing their livelihoods and maybe their homes. And on every Thursday evening at 8.00 p.m. we would turn out on our doorsteps and clap vigorously or clatter pans or saucepan lids or anything that made lots of noise, to show how much we appreciated the work done by our health workers and carers. We applauded those people, whose faces bore the pressure marks of wearing full Personal Protective Equipment for hours on end as they tried to manage lives, save lives. How grateful we felt towards our 'heroes'.

In the evenings we could watch 'From Our House To Your house', opera and ballet broadcast from the Royal Opera House, which was wonderful. We loved the beautiful music and light-hearted silliness of 'Cosi Fan Tutte', and the humour of 'La Fille Mal Gardée'. And of course the wonderfully creative five-minute 'Swan Lake' where most 'swans' danced in splendid isolation in their baths! We binged on Netflix 'The Crown'. My son, far from being in holiday mode, worked long hours as a delivery driver, starting early and ending late, elevated to 'key worker' status. He enjoyed crashing in front of the TV after a long and busy day.

How life changed in a flash

At the end of May a life-changing moment happened. It was a sunny day and I had pushed my daughter out in her chair for our daily walk. Returning home, I pulled her chair through our garden gate and there was a short lightning flash. I thought that I had caught a ray of strong sunshine over my sunglasses that had slipped down my nose. I pushed my daughter's chair up the wooden ramp and into our kitchen. My eyes were troubled by that strange darkness that we often experience when we come indoors from bright sunlight. But this was different. The shadow to the left side of my eyes persisted. I looked in the mirror of the sideboard and the left side of my face was in shadow. I tried to persuade myself it was the darkness of the room, but I knew something was wrong. I walked into the kitchen and saw only my daughter's body in her wheelchair, not her head. I moved my eyes and her head appeared. I saw swirling movements and waves around the left side of my eyes. A carer arrived and began painting my daughter's nails. My son came home early and I just sat there in my chair, utterly exhausted.

That night I was too afraid to go to bed until the swirls and waves at the side of my eyes had calmed somewhat. I fell asleep at about 3 a.m. During the next few days my eyes treated me to swirling wheels, jagged lights and swirling waves. They were also very light sensitive. I spoke to my optician who, like me, thought that this was a migraine without headache, like one I had had many years ago.

No normal migraine

One morning I woke up and all the swirling had stopped. Wonderful. I could get on with lots of overdue paperwork. The following morning I walked from the bedroom to the hallway. It looked different: the ceiling looked higher and it seemed more spacious. That was odd. I walked into the kitchen. I knew it was my kitchen but it looked quite different. Yet it wasn't. It was exactly the same. It felt like seeing it for the first time but knowing what it looked like. I boiled water in the kettle and made two mugs of tea. I poured milk into one of them and couldn't find the edge of the mug. The milk went down the side. I tried again and realised there was something wrong with my depth perception. This wasn't a migraine. I called my GP who sent me to Bournemouth Hospital Emergency department telling me over the phone that it sounded as though I had had a stroke. Fortunately, my son was available to give me a lift because I live about 40 minutes' drive from the hospital.

At Emergency my son had to leave me and I had to go in alone because of Covid rules. Staff were kind and attentive, a blood test was taken and I was ushered to a side cubicle where I lay back on the examination bed and waited for a doctor. Clinical examination and a CT scan confirmed that a stroke had occurred in the right occipital (visual) lobe of my brain. The loss of vision, termed a left upper quadrantonopia, is visual loss in the upper left quarter of each eye. I was fitted with a 72-hour heart monitor but because of Covid, they didn't carry out a full eye test or an echocardiogram. I was then sent to collect my prescription for standard post stroke medication. Covid rules forbade anyone to accompany me beyond the limits of the A & E department, so I had to find my way along unfamiliar corridors, twice taking wrong turns and feeling lost both within the building and myself.

Suddenly life was different. I was different. I had lost some visual field and with that some self image and self-confidence. I waited alone for my meds and emerged from the cavernous interior of the hospital to the comfort of my son and his car. He drove me back home. The hospital staff had been very nice and I told one nurse how impressed I was with the speed and efficiency with which I had been processed. She smiled and said "It's not usually like this. It's because of Covid, people aren't coming into hospital."

Scared to go to sleep

My 72-hour heart monitor was not read and reported on for three weeks. Another delay because of Covid. I tried to contact the cardiac department for information with no luck. I emailed the consultant whom I had seen in A & E, but no response, and my GP declined to make any enquiries on my behalf. It felt as though no one knew nor cared. I have never met the consultant in whose care I am supposed to be. I'm aware that I'm not alone in this and the pandemic has impacted hugely on the medical care and health of many.

I was fortunate to receive support from a Stroke rehabilitation community occupational therapist (OT) who accompanied me on a walk when I lacked confidence to go out alone. What a strange picture we made, she in her full PPE, apron billowing in the wind and me with a bright yellow peaked hat that belonged to my son, set at an angle to cover the left side of my eyes, dark sunglasses and a floral patterned walking stick in case I suddenly felt the need for support! Where I live you often don't see anybody when you leave the house, but on that day, the neighbours were out in force, jaws dropping at the sight that greeted them and too surprised to question me. The OT also used a scanning practice technique of blu-tacking playing cards to glass doors in my house to practice scanning speed. "Nine of clubs!" I'd shout or "Jack of hearts!" when she pointed at the next card. I'm not very competitive but found myself competing with myself, trying to prove how quickly I could see each card she pointed to. Scanning practice is vital for accommodation to this visual loss.

At night I was so afraid to go to bed. I didn't know whether I would still be able to see when I woke up. Would another stroke creep up in the night and happen without my knowledge, robbing me of my vision entirely? I stayed up till the early hours, listening to music and drinking hot chocolate, so much hot chocolate! No wonder my scales tell their own pandemic story! I had to sleep at some point, of course, and I often slept in the daytime too - post stroke fatigue, I'm told. When I finally turned out the light, I couldn't bear the darkness. I needed to know that I could see. So, I used a plug-in nightlight to provide a little ambient light. Almost one year on, I still do. The radio plays all night, at low volume, providing some sort of comfort.

At last, some good news

It took Social Services at least 10 days to respond to the change in my health and in the meantime, I was still providing full-time care for my daughter except for an hour and a half on five mornings. However, the subsequent care package was very helpful. We were so fortunate to have carers available to support us throughout. For that I have felt immensely grateful.

For three months during the pandemic I was not allowed to drive. It helped that there was nowhere to go! There was the prospect that I might not ever drive again. I spent many days worrying about where I live - a car and driver are indispensable here. I began to look for houses in a nearby city, so certain was I that driving days were over. I gazed sadly at my driving licence knowing that I would have to return it. Finally a visual field test was carried out, four months after the stroke, and the result was good. I have a good enough visual field to pass the DVLA test and continue to drive. The taxi driver who had taken me to my hospital appointment was as pleased as I was at the result though I pointed out that it wasn't good for his business!!

Spring lawn

All the colours of spring

And now, spring is here and the latest lockdown is easing. Sunshine is working magic on my garden, encouraging a mass of daffodils to bloom; the paler yellow of primrose encroaching on the grass, deep vibrant pinks of camellia bushes, pale pinks and whites of magnolia trees and shrubs, the blues of comfrey and periwinkle, and many hellebores facing earthwards, hiding their blooms. They need to be brought indoors to float in a bowl of water facing upwards to display their beauty. And I can see them all. Soon there will be places to go, and I can drive to them.

As lockdown restrictions ease and life opens up again, my personal health journey through Covid leaves me far less restricted than I had thought it might. I remain plagued by post stroke fatigue but hope, the good weather, more activity, and more people in real life will help me back to my pre pandemic energy. I feel more fortunate than many.

Hellebores

Nineteen

15 What is the acronym for face, hands and body covering which offers some protection from disease?

Questions

(ANSWERS IN BACK OF BOOK)

Working from home

Working from home and having the kids off school seemed fun at first - for a week or so. But try doing your job as an editor and supervising the schoolwork of an eight-year old and a 13-year old at the same time... In the end, I worked mostly at night when they were in bed. I don't think I've ever been so exhausted in my life.'

Katherine

In dedication

For all the NHS staff who have worked tirelessly and selflessly, under immense pressure, to look after our nation throughout 2020. I cannot thank them enough.

Jane Macario

Lockdown Pets

Luna

Sophie - Miniature Dachshund

Smokie - Toy Poodle

Oscar - Burmese

Oscar - British Shorthair cross

Crumble - Golden Retriever

Cosmo - French Bulldog

Jess - Jackapoo

A lesson in resilience

I was really emotional waving goodbye to my class on Friday 20th March 2020 not knowing when or if I would ever teach them again. After weeks of wondering 'Will they..? Won't they...?' We'd been given two days notice by Boris Johnson that schools were not safe and were going to close. Three days later we were in a national lockdown. I thought it would only be for a few weeks, but like the rest of the nation, I had no idea what the following year was going to hold.

The next few months were surreal. I settled into this new world of working from home, something I never imagined I would do as a teacher. My days consisted of planning, uploading work, recording video messages and communicating with my class through emails. I received messages from tired and worried parents detailing their days of juggling work and home schooling. I received cards from the children in my class telling me how much they missed school and their friends. We were all trying to navigate this strange new normal together yet we weren't allowed to actually be together in school.

I loved the weeks that I was on rota in school. It felt nice to be back in the familiar surroundings... even though they were very quiet and empty. Teaching a small group of Key Worker children ranging from Year R to Year 6 had its huge challenges but in between the lessons, we spent the days doing Joe Wicks workouts, building dens and trying to make it fun when everything felt so strange.

Then came June. I was in a routine of setting work to my class remotely but, like many other teachers and parents, waiting desperately for an announcement about when the children could return. We soon heard there would be a phased return and that Years R, 1 and 6 could go back to school. I was gutted that my year 2 class still had to stay at home. We continued to develop our remote learning and began weekly class video calls. The children beamed as they waved to their friends online, they listened intently as I read stories and it was complete chaos as they ran round their houses during scavenger hunts! We had great fun, but it still wasn't the same as being in school together.

At our school, all children returned for the last four weeks of summer term on a part-time basis. Although this meant only half of the class could be in at a time, I was so excited to have my class back. The sight of the smiles on their faces as they walked into their classroom and saw their friends is something I will never forget. We had lots of fun in those last few weeks and just enjoyed each other's company again.

Fast forward to September and the start of a new school year and a new class. From September to December, although we were in another lockdown and many people were furloughed, life felt quite normal for me. All the children were back at school and we were in full swing of supporting catch up of the missed curriculum. Things were different this year though... children sitting in rows, no school assemblies in the hall, no singing, no school trips, parents' evening over video call, no nativity performance - and we washed our hands a whole lot more. That didn't stop us having fun. We enjoyed video call assemblies, live streamed music performances to parents at home and had a socially distanced visit from Santa at Christmas. We tried our best to carry on as normally as we could despite the worry of a potential positive COVID case constantly looming over us.

I reached the Christmas holidays with a sigh of relief. Feeling lucky that my class had survived the term with no isolation closures, knowing that unfortunately this hadn't been the case for other classes. As for most people, Christmas 2020 was very different. The usual festivities were limited and it was soon announced that we were moving into another national lockdown. We wondered if the schools would close again...

The holidays came to an end and we returned to school on Monday 4th January. Despite the restrictions, the children excitedly shared stories about the fun they had had over the break. We spent our staff meeting that evening planning for a potential future lockdown, not knowing that only hours later, Boris would announce that schools were closing that very next morning.

Those next few days and weeks were really, really tough. This felt much harder than the first lockdown. The children had already missed so much of their education and the expectations of remote teaching had increased. With only 11 hours to prepare, it was now my responsibility to provide the curriculum to my class at home and to a group of Key Worker children in school... at times this felt like an impossible challenge. There were so many tears but as a staff team, we got through it one day at a time.

We spent hours preparing lessons to upload online. We taught in class at the same time as teaching those at home via video call. The children at home were fantastic and desperate to spend time with their schoolmates. I felt so proud of my class for their resilience, enthusiasm and effort. Again, we had settled into this new way of living and it had become our new normal.

On the 8th March, schools in England reopened to all children and we have now enjoyed our first few weeks back together. The children seem so grateful and happy to be back within our school community. With the rollout of the vaccine and COVID testing in school, I feel hopeful that the end is in sight. I hadn't reflected on the impact of COVID on my life until now. I have been on a massive journey with the two classes I taught this year, and it is an experience I will never forget.

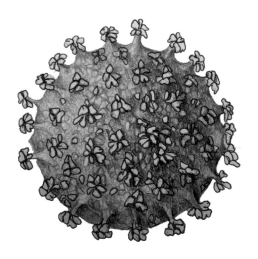

Covid Botanical illustration
by Jenny Malcolm

A perfect storm

I left the UK in February 2020 to teach paramedics in Vanuatu for two months. I had been two years before to this peaceful and beautiful country and was looking forward to an interesting trip. Vanuatu became independent in 1980. It is comprised of 65 inhabited islands in the South Pacific. 1500 miles East of Australia it is about as far as you can travel from the UK and is truly a tropical paradise. I was to be based on Espiritu Santo, the largest island, about the size of Somerset where I normally live. Covered in tropical rain forest with a small population and very little infrastructure I loved it from the moment I first saw it.

I had heard of COVID before I left the UK and the WHO declared it a pandemic as I was traveling. As a paramedic in my late 60s I was concerned that there were only two ventilators in the islands. On the plus side the islands were remote and had no known cases. It certainly seemed a safer place than the UK at that time.

By mid-March the government of Vanuatu had passed an emergency powers act. All ferries and flights had been cancelled with the islands locked down and WHO precautions put into place. I was volunteering for an Australian charity and all the Australian volunteers had to leave. I made enquiries about my flights and if I was allowed to transit Australia. I was told, at first, that my flights would leave and then I was told that they would not leave. By the end of March I knew that my flight to Port Vila would not leave and later that my international flights had been cancelled.

This left me in a difficult situation. My visa ran out 31st March and the rules said that to renew it I had to leave the country for at least 24 hours. As if that wasn't difficult enough news came in that COVID had reached the Solomon Islands, Fiji and Noumea. That was it; I was stuck with no way out. I turned to the Foreign and Commonwealth Office whose replies to my questions never seemed to have any relevance and then the British High Commission in Port Villa. At last, I had found somebody who understood the problem. They could make no promises but had contacts with other embassies who were all trying to get their expats home.

With my mental state improved I was happy to stay doing the job I had come to do. I had three students with me and 24 hours a day to provide paramedic ambulance cover for the whole island. As the only person with qualifications, I had to be on call to give necessary drugs, but the workload was not too high at that time.

From the beginning of April, a tropical cyclone called Harold started to form in the Solomon Islands. It killed eight people capsizing a boat but was several hundred miles away from our location. The days went by and the warning system started to send texts to our phones telling of the slowly increasing wind speed. By the 5th April Harold had slowed its progress across the ocean but increased to category 5, the highest rating for a storm like this. Twice in the night Harold turned 180 degrees out of the way towards Santo and twice it turned and came straight for us.

At dawn it was clearly going to be stormy. Two hours later the full force hit. Gusts over 200 mph hit like hammer blows. The rain was equally spectacular with 20 inches falling in 6 hours. To start with bits of wood struck the building I was living in. This was followed by corrugated iron roofing sheets flying by and lastly by full sized trees being torn out of the ground. My room was shaking with the roof vibrating and the rain forcing through cracks around the window frames. Everything I possessed was wet and I had taken shelter on a steel framed bunk bed for my own safety.

I have been shot at and blown up in war zones, but never have I been so frightened as by this display of the force of nature. That night was very dark with no electricity and no water, apart from the paddling pool I now lived in. No phones were working, and no radio stations were broadcasting. For the first time in my life I felt home sick. I have been traveling for a large part of my life but I have always known when I would get home. That night I wasn't sure I would get back.

The next day saw the start of the disaster relief effort. The whole Southern half of the island was destroyed. Buildings, trees, boats and cars were all damaged. A rescue team was sent from Vila to help our ambulances get through blocked roads and we started the difficult task of finding injured people in the remote areas of rain forest and getting them to hospital. Many stories came out of the story of Harold. One village broke a hole in the concrete rainwater storage tank and started to load their children into it. The idea was to safeguard the children whilst the adults took their chances in a collapsing community hall.

It took months to get back to any sense of normality and the damage will take a long time to repair. More than 40 schools were destroyed and plans for cyclone proof replacements were designed but have not yet been funded.

I worked every day treating patients and eventually got my visa sorted out. The visa office had been destroyed but they found a replacement. With government permission I finally got a cargo flight to Auckland and arrived in the UK at the end of October.

Nich Woolf with passenger who is about to give birth to triplets!

The final surprise was the award of a British Empire Medal for services to emergency medicine and disaster relief in the New Year's Honours. 2020 - a year in my life I will never forget.

Nich Woolf

Songs by David Younger

Here are a couple of COVID-related songs I wrote & recorded during 2020 - expressing feelings of:

1) Disappointment ('Question') at selfish behaviour & poor citizenship displayed by some people

2) Anger ('Hypocrisy & Heroes') towards political figures, coupled with great respect for the many 'heroes' of COVID

QUESTION - What it's about?

All around the world there hangs a question
To all with friends & family around them
To everybody blessed with creature comforts
Can we try & be more humanitarian?

We'll see if we will learn that lonely lives deserve a moment to be recognised.
We'll see if we can step away from our own lives

Now it feels we've reached a crossroad
A chance to see that selfishness runs far & wide
A need for us to show far more compassion
But can we cast self-centredness aside?

We'll see if we can learn that poverty deserves a moment to be recognised

We'll see if we can mend our ways in time

Scan the QR code to listen to 'Question' online

HYPOCRISY & HEROES

You're making all the news
Your broken rules are clear for all to see
Weakly justified
With arrogance & hypocrisy

With heroes all around
People of immense integrity
The injustice of it all
Lies told free of anxiety
Like a book, don't think we can't read you
You're transparent

Self-prepared support
And shocking governmental puppetry
With no hint of remorse
You've reached new depths of toxicity

See the heroes all around
Heart-warming displays of bravery
The injustice of it all
Souls lost alone in a human tragedy
Like a book, don't think we can't read you
Your judgement was so wrong

Scan the QR code to listen to 'Hypocrisy & Heroes' online

Barbara's story

Thursday 5th November

Today, I went over to the Macmillan Unit in Christchurch as usual, only this time it was to say goodbye to my husband David. I knew it was only a matter of hours or days. I kissed him on the forehead and told him it was okay to go... I don't know if he realised I was there. David had been ill with prostate cancer for eighteen months and we had agreed that he would stay at home as long as possible. I had been his carer for the last few months of his life.

I did not sleep that night and at 6 a.m. I went out into the garden. A lone star in the dark morning sky was twinkling at me... I guessed it was David saying 'It's okay, Babs, I've gone.' I climbed back into bed with Lottie, our crazy boxer dog, lying on David's side.

Babs

Friday 6th November
At 8.a.m. the call came that David had passed away at 6.14 a.m. that

morning. My best friend and husband of 42 years was gone. They asked me to come to the Unit sooner rather than later, as there was only one other patient on the ward and it was obviously not nice for this man to lie there with someone who had just died. He must be thinking: 'My turn next...'

I got dressed and went to say goodbye to David once more. Security was even more strict than usual. Now I had to mask up, gel up and even put on a plastic apron before going through the locked doors to the unit. My daughter Siobhan, son-in-law Paul, and grandchildren had rushed down from Basingstoke to take me there; I was too emotional to drive. Siobhan could not go in to say goodbye; only one family member was allowed in. I was pleased, in a way: the man in the bed was no longer her dad – he was long gone, there was only the shell of the man I had loved so much.

I spent the weekend trying to plan the funeral. It had to be limited to twenty people because of COVID-19. It was one of the most difficult things I have ever had to do; I had always thought I would be the first to go.

Monday 9th November

The family came to take me to the Macmillan Unit to pick up David's belongings. There had been an outbreak of Coronavirus on Thursday and they were shutting down all the wards. I was fine, apart from a small tickly cough, but as I am always a bit chesty, I thought nothing of it. Once the family had left, I climbed into bed, switched off from the world and just cried. At that time a friend's son was doing some gardening work for me, and apparently his spade had sliced through the Virgin cable. I had no Internet, no landline, no Wi-Fi, but what did I care? David was gone; how was I going to go on without him?

The verdict

The next few days were a bit of a blur. I had phoned the doctor and asked for some antibiotics for my chesty cough and a friend picked them up from the chemist and dropped them by my door. I stopped answering my mobile. Nothing mattered to me; I just wanted the world to stop so that I could jump off. In the end, my son-in-law Paul got through to me. He turned up with a large bag of food and a finger pulse oxygen reader. From then on he phoned me every day to get the readings. They were consistently low, so he urged me to get tested for COVID-19. Somewhere around day three I left my bed and drove to St Pauls Lane to be checked. I was in such a foggy mental state that I drove up the pavement twice.

Back home I curled up with Lottie and cried. My world was falling apart, and I was on my own in the house and could not look after myself, let alone Lottie. The NHS message came through two days later saying: You have tested Positive for Covid-19. Please stay in isolation for 10 days...

What was I to do? First of all I had to cancel the funeral, the flowers and the printers. The local Funeral Directors dealt with everything in the most patient, diplomatic and compassionate way. After that, all I wanted to do was hide under the covers.

Singing spiders

It started with a lower back pain, then it moved up, and I started aching all over. I had no energy even to get out of bed to feed the dog or spend a penny. My breathing was very laboured and I had no taste or smell. All I could think was: 'I just want to be with David, so I don't care if I live or die.'

I took two Paracetamol and fell asleep. When I woke up, my nightshirt was so soaking wet that I could wring it out and my hair had droplets dripping off the ends... It felt like I had climbed into a bath of cold water with my clothes on and then gone straight to bed. All mobile calls went unanswered; my poor sister from Dublin did not know if I was alive or dead. Some friends discussed getting in touch with Social Services. No one knew what was happening, only Paul and the Funeral Directors.

Then the hallucinations began. I looked at the ceiling light and saw large black smiling spiders climb out. They began to build a web ladder and climbed down with outstretched legs. They pulled me out of bed and carried me up to the light, and we danced around the light fitting singing 'Ring a Ring a Roses'. Strangely enough, I was not scared.

Once friends and family knew what was happening, they rallied round with food parcels – all left by the door. There were home cooked meals, flowers, chocolates. Baileys, soup... Masses were being said for David and bereavement cards and get-well cards began to arrive. I scanned them without really seeing the words or noticing who they were from.

When the worst hallucinations were over, I went downstairs to find at least two days of doggie poo in the lounge and dining room, along with dried-in wee. I couldn't believe it. Poor dog; not only had she lost her best friend in the whole world, her Daddy David, but what the hell was happening to her Mummy?

I had not eaten for ten days or been to the toilet properly. I remember lying on the cold bathroom tiles, sobbing. I was like an old fortress with solid drawbridge doors: nothing could get in or out. It was the most horrible experience. I phoned the doctor, who sent a prescription to the surgery, which another great friend picked up and dropped by my door. That brought relief, finally.

My oxygen levels remained around 88/89 so Paul insisted I telephone 111, which I did... They gave me a two-hour window before an ambulance would come to pick me up. I packed an overnight bag and some friends came to pick up Lottie. I did not know what lay ahead or how long I would be in hospital. At least the funeral was on hold for the moment.

Angels and demons

In hospital I was taken to the Acute Medical Ward. From then, everything happened fast. After an X-ray, a scan and a number of tests I was transferred to Ward 14 where I was given my own room. I was happy: I had my own en-suite toilet, and a young Filipino nurse called John set me up with a TV. I didn't sleep much that night, but I did feel safe. I was finally in the right place.

The following morning I was feeling much better and even looked forward to some porridge. Later, there were more tests, more forms to fill in... and the news that I had to move next door, to a women's bay with six beds. They had a gentleman arriving and did not want to put him in with the ladies. So off I was wheeled to the larger ward. It should have had a sign over the door: 'You are now entering another world'.

Three beds on the left and three beds on the right, with me in the middle on the left. They wanted a better oxygen reading, so they were going to inject into my wrist. 'This is really going to hurt,' said the young nurse. I thought she was joking: I had a cannula in my left arm and a bigger one in my right. I had been a blood donor for over twenty years... a needle is a needle, right? Wrong. Normally I don't cry out in pain, but this was like no other injection before as it sank into my veins... As I cried and almost died with the pain, the Hospital Radio Bedside played 'Things can only get Better' By D:Ream...

That night was sheer hell. The elderly lady to my right cried like a banshee throughout the night, the lady opposite me was screaming for a banana at 1.30.a.m. The following morning was not much better: the lady to my right kept pulling at her oxygen tube and was bleeding. The lady opposite me wanted a bedpan, started to climb out of bed and fell to the floor. Before I knew it, six members of staff were closing the screens around her bed and, with the help of a hastily brought in blow-up bed, managed to get her into her own bed. When the screens were opened she was lying there in her bed looking regal... I wondered who she was in real life and put her down as some high-flying CEO of some big company. Amazing what ill health can do to you.

The pretty nurse who had told me my injection would hurt was on duty. She was the daughter every mother would wish for. We talked about COVID and how she had to wash her hair – beautiful cornrows around her head - every day. She also told me she had to pay £ 7 each day to park at the hospital. My blood pressure nearly went through the roof. I will never forget her for as long as I live. She was so suited to her job, and I was grateful for the warmth and compassion she showed at such a difficult time. If I had to choose an angel on earth that day, it would have to be her.

After three days in hospital, I no longer had COVID-19. Clearly, I had suffered the worst of it at home. I could pick up where I had left off, but I was dreading what lay ahead. I sorted out David's obituary, the songs and verses we would have at the service, and who would be invited. The funeral was rebooked for December 4th..

And now?

So here we are in early January 2021 – about six weeks down the road and my sense of smell and taste are still gone. My energy is about 85% and getting there. My bladder is still weak and my muscle mass has not returned… being in bed for almost 13 days, along with taking steroids have had an effect on my health. I still have a lung nodule and am waiting for a follow-up appointment to check this out.

Trying to deal with life without David and then COVID-19 makes 2020 the worst year of my life. But I try to count my blessings. I think of all the other people out there who are older than me, on their own and living in fear – how frightening it must be for them.

I'm playing by the rules. I don't see my family; I don't get to hug my lovely grandchildren Noah and Isla. I keep myself to myself and do two small local shops a week. I walk Lottie daily, which helps both of us.

I can only hope and pray that when people in the future look back on this time, they, too, will understand that 2020 was the year when we finally realised what the important things in life are. Family, friends, and looking after our Planet. Without these, life is not worth living.

Barbara J. Fowler

Artwork by Luke Gevell

Covid and me – It's a dogs life

By Brinkley, age 15 months (March 2020)

Mum suddenly was always **HOME**, with me, awesome pawsome! We went on lovely long walks **EVERY** day and the sun was always shining. Although it did seem that we went on the same walks, the same fields, the same rabbits who knew when to hide when they saw me, silly rabbits! When we saw other mums and dads they didn't come and say hello to me though, like they used too. Mum said we had to keep a "distance", I'm not sure I like this distance malarkey, I like jumping up and putting my muddy paws everywhere, but mum says I shouldn't do that anyway, that's what **DOWN** means.

Brinkley

I don't really understand what a car is, but when mum shouts **CAR** I have to stop and sit. This hasn't happened much lately, It's been nice not having to have my lead pulled and to have to sit still FOREVER when I KNOW there are pheasants to chase up ahead, pheasants love being chased by me!

Brinkley - ready for walkies!

Mum likes cuddles more now too, apparently mum isn't allowed to cuddle anyone, apart from Bubble. I'm still not quite sure who Bubble is as we haven't had many visitors lately, I think Mum misses that, so I try to give her even more cuddles to make up for it.

The bestest thing though is that I am now a "saviour" and it has been such fun! It's something to do with mum saying I had to be on my **BESTEST** behaviour and then these little people came into my life, not small like me, but not BIG like mum. They taught me about balls and sticks! Apparently me being their friend and going on lovely long walks with them has really helped them and their mum during this thing called lockdown. It's kinda cool being a saviour and sticks are now my **FAVOURITE** things!

Mum says that one day things will be back to normal. I don't know what normal is, I just know that I love things now, just the way they are.

Zooming good fun

They say you can't teach an old dog new tricks and although I don't like to describe myself as an 'old dog', I have definitely struggled with the 'new tricks'!

Before 23rd March 2020, my job involved some days visiting schools and working with children with special educational needs and other days going into my office to write up reports. Suddenly, overnight, schools and offices were closed and I was instructed to work at home, go on virtual training courses, attend virtual meetings, deliver virtual training and teach children online! I, along with many others, was totally out of my comfort zone. Very quickly, I had to learn how to use Zoom and Microsoft TEAMS to do my job.

In some ways it was lovely to roll out of bed an hour later in the mornings, put my tracksuit bottoms and slippers on, walk to the spare room (my office), switch on the computer and enjoy the extra online training courses available.

Apart from learning so much, it was comforting to know that everyone had the same hurdles to overcome and there were a few memorable moments during training sessions. For example, the time when the speaker, Daphne, who fortunately could be heard but not seen, suddenly fell quiet after an audible loud scraping noise during her training on Dyscalculia and said "I'm terribly sorry everyone, I just fell off my chair!" Or during another course when the view on our screens switched to a speaker who was obviously taken by surprise because her husband (I presume) was standing behind her with a basket full of dirty washing. He froze, thinking we wouldn't notice, but when he realised he was stuck there and she would be speaking for some time, he very slowly edged out of view. Sadly, I remember these entertaining moments with much greater clarity than the content of the training!

However, the boot was on the other foot when I found myself in a very uncomfortable position during training I was co-delivering. Two of my colleagues and I were presenting a course to a group of 25 teachers. It was training we had newly devised, we each had a section to present and we were rather nervous about it. One of my colleagues has a wealth of expertise and experience in the subject matter and was leading the middle 'meaty' part of the delivery. She was also in charge of sharing the power point from her computer. I had finished my section and passed on to her. All seemed to be going swimmingly. Suddenly, after her initial few words, she 'froze' on our screens and disappeared as her internet failed, leaving my other colleague and me to complete the 30 remaining minutes of training. PANIC! We waited a few seconds in disbelief, trying to decide what to do and then attempted to pick up the pieces. I shared my screen but my brain and fingers stopped working and I couldn't remember how to do it, eventually getting a much smaller version of the power point on our screens. My other colleague then did a marvellous job of squinting at the power point and talking through the slides, pretending to know what she was talking about. I'd like to say that no one noticed but I'm pretty sure that wasn't the case.

Suddenly, I had a huge amount of sympathy for Daphne and her chair incident! In my house, the door to the shower room is right next to 'my office' in the spare room.

Initially, my son had to crawl behind my chair, dragging his clothes with him, to get to the shower in the morning if I was in a meeting. Apart from the off-putting drone of the power shower, this worked quite well until one of my colleagues commented on the fact that the door next to me appeared to open on it's own. We now have a system whereby he knocks gently when he needs to get to the shower and I switch off my microphone and slowly move my chair and direct the screen away from the shower door and tell him when the coast is clear, then he can just walk normally as he did in the good old days before lockdown.

I have found that it is difficult to focus on the content of meetings that take place virtually. I find myself studying everyone's homes. Straining to see the colour of their curtains, what is on the shelf behind them, or how tidy their kitchens are. As a result, I spend five minutes before every meeting tidying the area of bedroom behind me.

However, as time has gone on, we have all got wise to this and have learnt how to blur our backgrounds or even change them to a scene of a tropical beach or The Statue of Liberty.

The most common phrases in any meeting this past year have been, in reverse order:

3) "I can't wait until we can meet face to face"
2) "Can you hear me?"
1) "You're on mute!"

However, if I had to choose my favourite moment from a virtual meeting, it would have to be the time when one person in a meeting of 127 people, who obviously thought she had switched her microphone off, shouted "Can you take the fish out of the microwave?"

So, at the end of a rather stressful and physically inactive working day in 'my office', it has been good to stretch, move and keep fit. The benefits of my regular Pilates classes have been a life saver. But of course, restrictions have meant that there are no live classes and they too, require me to be in front of a screen, in Zoom classes. AAAAAAAAAAAHHHHHHHH!

Again, there are frequent blips when someone's internet fails or when they can't find the button to mute! However, there was a particularly memorable high spot during one class when halfway through, the husband of one of the class members walked behind her and upstairs wearing nothing but his underpants! Very distracting (and rather exciting) for all of us....not least the instructor who had to stop the class while she composed herself. Inspecting the semi-naked man in the background on screen certainly beats straining to see how tidy their rooms are!

All in all....it's been Zooming good fun!

Nineteen

16 Questions

What is a form or version of an infectious disease that differs from other forms?

(ANSWERS IN BACK OF BOOK)

When this is all over

When this is all over I will sigh a long sigh and say Thank You to someone, I don't know who. I shall wonder afresh who made everything. If I look carefully I shall see things I never saw before that were always there despite me not seeing.

When this is all over I shall look at things more carefully and cherish them slowly before rushing on. I shall look at the pattern on my carpet and wonder whose hand drew it, what their favourite food was, whether they preferred Bach to the Beatles. If they had a cat what type it would be.

When this is all over I shall appreciate the infinite wonder in a bowl of porridge. How could I have missed it all before? I shall like things I always took for granted before. I shall ask myself how many people it takes to imagine, invent, engineer, design, redesign, check, convince, plan, mass produce, assemble, package and distribute my not-so-simple Oyster Card.

When this is all over I will read books and wonder what the author had for breakfast when this page was written, whether they had to let the dog out to bark at squirrels, whether they had a package delivered, or suddenly noticed that their tulips were dropping their petals.

When this is all over I will make a weather-proof sign saying Thank You and stick it on my wheelie bin. I am practising my new smile now so that I can give it to lots of people who don't know me. I shall be grateful that 'lockdown' has made me more familiar with all the things I stuffed in my house and hardly knew I had.

When this is all over I will remember how beautiful roads were when there were hardly any cars on them. I will wonder who the people are who run the traffic lights. How many lorries are delivering food, medical supplies, oxygen, toys and bathmats right now. I shall gaze at the dust in a sunbeam and wonder who is passing by today.

When this is all over I will count my steps as I walk and be thankful that these are steps I might have been robbed of by something as simple sounding as a pandemic. Trees and flowers will be my special friends. Birdsong will be my best music. And rolling blue skies will make me look up and keep saying

Thank You, Michael Sherman 04/2020

This poem was introduced by Gill Kaye Editor of Ingenue Arts and Culture Magazine www.ingenuemagazine.co.uk
And used with kind permission of Michael Sherman

Family matters

It hit me when I was talking to my 10 year old granddaughter, Grace, who said "Graneeee, that was back in the real life" she was referring to 2019/early 2020. Yes indeed, that was 'real life' as we knew it then ......

Above all things, I am a mother, doting grandmother, wife, sister and, I hope, a good friend. And what I have missed more than anything is the contact, the embraces, the one to ones and the sharing of experiences.

But two very positive things have come out of 'not real life' or shall we say 'lockdown life' in our expanding family unit:

The first being a 'lockdown love affair' between our third son Joseph and a very passionate Italian girl Dany who came to visit him in the UK for 10 days at the beginning of March and they have been in a relationship ever since! She arrived very nervously to a welcome dinner with our entire family; and now she is very much part of our family. Due to various work and family commitments they have been isolating now in the UK, Italy and Majorca and it looks like a strong meaningful relationship has been formed. Joseph has been making attempts to learn Italian and Dany is trying to give up coffee and complaining about cold UK temperatures.

As both our younger sons were home with us for a period of time during lockdown, we discovered fire pits and the fun of eating 'al fresco' with rugs around our knees. We enjoyed long conversations, gardening and indulging in a variety of cooking talents. We spent many a visit on the outdoor balcony and birthday cakes were made and eaten with no candles being blown but all the sentiment was there! I found it very hard to see our granddaughters through windows and peering over fences, all I wanted to do was get hold of them and give them a great big HUG! They have morphed into giraffes as they have become so tall and I feel I have missed so much of their precious growing years.

The second wonderful thing to happen was in-between lockdown one and two, our eldest son Marcus and his partner Emma announced that they were expecting. They had been trying to conceive for some time so we were bursting with excitement when they rang and announced the news of twins, a boy and a girl due in April 2021. I wonder what they will be named?

Personally, I have experienced highs and not too many lows during lockdown. As well as working in our family business, I rediscovered my artistic side, making, decorating and writing. However, January arrives and I don't feel much like emerging from the cocoon of my duvet - what for? Sad news, grey skies, no particular motivation. I quickly remind myself how lucky I am not to have had a serious grieving due to this wretched virus. Unfortunately, I have shared with others close to me who have. I think of all those wonderful people out there saving lives; keeping the world functioning. I feel very small but, in the scheme of things, I am very small. I can only be proud of doing my bit to keep myself and my family safe and not burdening the NHS.

As a family, we are blessed to have two new additions to look forward to next year. In twenty years' time, they may well be reading this book as a historic happening and will be intrigued by its very contents. I myself wonder what kind of world will be out there for them to enjoy?

Clare Lee (family person)

The Covid lockdown couple

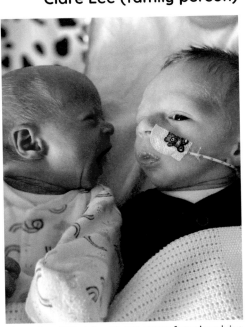

The twins. Kiki giving Kenzo some female advice

The worst of times, the best of times

Like most of us, I think, I found it difficult to actually believe we were seriously entering a lockdown. The things that were being said were no different from what I had heard about Sars, Ebola, Swine Flu and other diseases. Even later, when the lockdown was upon us, it still didn't sound plausible that a man could eat a bat bought in a market on the other side of the world with such serious consequences for the rest of the world. How wrong I was.

Initially, there was shock, genuine shock that it was happening. I was out for the afternoon when the Prime Minister made the announcement that we must all stay at home. I had been playing squash and was about to enjoy a post-game drink. The atmosphere in my club was like I had never experienced before; people were bewildered, disbelieving and angry. There was widespread bemusement and a sense of worry too. There was, of course, some gallows humour and we said our farewells with a cheery "see you in three weeks". (Or at least, as cheery as we could manage in the circumstances).

So then... reading the papers, listening to the news and following events on social media. Early on I read something to the effect that there would never be a better time to achieve something you had never got around to doing. In other words, if you didn't get it done during lockdown then the problem wasn't lack of time – as you had been telling yourself – it was YOU. Like many of us, I read about Albert Camus and his now in-vogue book. And I witnessed the behaviour of people in shops and supermarkets. Even now, I recall a woman in the supermarket striding purposefully toward the virtually empty shelves. She reached up and put the two remaining whole chickens into a bag (there were no baskets or trollies to be seen) and walked off leaving the shelf completely bare. Then she strode over to the chill cabinet and did the exact same thing to the few remaining slices of cold meat and a couple of pizzas. She didn't even look at what she was stuffing into her bag. I'll probably never forget it. I got home and it dawned on me that we were about to witness both the very best and the very worst of human behaviour. 'Choose wisely', I thought to myself.

Love your neighbours

I tried to figure out what I could or should do with all this time that was about to present itself to me. I went through the usual things: lose weight, run daily, declutter the house, get the garden looking immaculate... all the things most people promised themselves. I also added some weirder stuff that this might be the right time to attempt: learn to play a musical instrument, teach myself Turkish or Japanese or something, take up yoga... all the things you admire in others but think 'this isn't for me'.

And I gave it serious thought, I really did.

I love the road I live on. In the summer following the murder of MP Jo Cox, we had a lovely street party as we embraced the 'Great Together', the highlight of which was a huge tug of war contest between the odds and the evens (the odds won, 2-1) and we decided to repeat the event on the following Boxing Day, with mince pies and hip flasks to replace the nachos and cold beer. It came as no surprise, therefore, that before long a neighbour set up a WhatsApp group for the street. Suddenly, people with whom I had only ever exchanged a friendly 'good morning' had names, house numbers and a personality for me. We shared information about planned shopping trips, we made lists of what we needed or had too much of, people offered to help each other and in a weird way it seemed like life was better, not worse. Fifteen months on and we still do it – and I look back on it as one of those "best of human behaviour' things I knew I would see.

One phone call a day

I kept pondering what I could do to make myself useful. It occurred to me that if neighbours could spare the time to offer help and support to people they barely knew then what about all those whom I already knew but rarely spoke with? I've been fortunate enough to have met lots of lovely people and I sort of stayed in touch with a good number of them. But, apart from the occasional Facebook exchange or Christmas card (remember them?) I rarely spoke with them. Decision made then! I would try to ring a different old friend every day. I was realistic enough to know that I wouldn't be able to do it every day due to other commitments (trying to earn a living somehow, elderly parents to look in on, etc.) but I figured that if I couldn't find half an hour to call someone I hadn't spoken to in a while then I should have a word with myself. And so, I began… My contacts list goes back years, so it really wasn't difficult. Old school friends, work colleagues from twenty or thirty years ago, golf partners from yesteryear, my university mates, former clients, friends from the various networks I've been a part of, distant family members were all in there. And so I began. And I am so pleased I did.

I have had some truly fabulous conversations with some lovely people. We've shared stories about the paths our lives have taken since we shared an office, or a locker room, or a lecture theatre. We've caught up on family, other colleagues, work, careers… you name it. Conversations have, of course, ranged from the trivial and the funny to the deeply moving and the thought provoking. Not everyone was always able to speak, and one or two needed several attempts and voicemail exchanges but they were all worth it. I can say that without exception, everyone was pleased to hear from me (or at least, that's what they told me) and we laughed, joked, swore, gasped, wept in abundance. It has been a really rewarding time.

Andy Parker

I've rekindled friendships and reminded myself how fortunate I was to have these people in my life. I've also learned a bit about myself, I hope.

These phone calls have lit up my life this past year or so. Early in lockdown, I could see there were aspects of my life that I loved, and others that I did for no better reason than habit. The steep learning curve of remote working now meant I could, if I were sensible, retain much of what I enjoy about life whilst also doing less of what didn't bring me joy. My phone call routine helped me realise that; it taught me that the meaningful is more important than the material and this will be a central pillar in my future life. I'm so pleased I did it.

Finally, for anyone still reading this and wondering... my weight is pretty much the same, I run and cycle no more than before, I never did learn a musical instrument or a foreign language, and no great new adventures have been undertaken.

On the plus side, the house has been well and truly decluttered (thank you, Marie Kondo, and I hope you're proud) and I am now a keen yoga devotee.

Andy Parker June 2021

In dedication

For breaking the silence with your calls
For breaking the loneliness with your messages
For breaking the boredom with your talks and the isolation with your walks
For saving me from breaking
To my friends and family at home and across the waters.
For your love and support.
Thank you x

EPM

Raise a glass to the future

Amy and Ian run The White Hart, a pub in the tiny village of Chilsworthy in Cornwall. The three hundred year old building is much more than a place to come for a pint: it is a social hub, where locals meet, where weddings and funerals are celebrated and where people even come to shop for essentials. One local called it the key to the community, and the rest of the village would agree. But in order to make the place more economically viable, Amy and Ian contacted Tom Kerridge and his programme 'Saving Britain's Pubs'. Amy had an idea to pull down an inside wall and make the best of the stunning view of the beautiful Cornish countryside. Tom agreed with this idea and also suggested that the couple should delegate more of their workload and should reconfigure the pub kitchen. They went ahead. And then Covid happened.

Celebrity chef Tom Kerridge outside The White Hart with Amy and Ian

Amy: "We bought the pub in September 2017 and we knew we had to do something to go forward and make it a viable business. We wanted to be there for the locals, but it's only a tiny village. We're not on a through-road so we don't get any passing trade; we needed people to know about us. That's why we contacted the show. Even before Covid happened, when making plans to knock down a wall, it was very stressful because of the money we were spending. It was scary. When Covid became a real threat and lockdown happened in March, it was like the end of our world. It felt as if we would never be able to open the front door of the pub again. Before furlough we also didn't know what sort of support we would get; it was devastating. The pub has been there for hundreds of years, it was open during the two World Wars and it was the first time it was shut.

We've always been here for the community and it was the strangest feeling: as soon as the door closed you lost the soul of the pub. It was cold and empty. We live upstairs and it was upsetting to be there; our lives changed overnight. One night we're buzzing with lovely customers having a great time, the next night it's just an empty old building. It was like a being in ghost town.

At the very beginning, and throughout the first lockdown, we sometimes thought of giving up. It was so hard. People said: 'It must be amazing, lockdown in a pub!' But it was the loneliest place you could be!

The White Hart

heart attack in November, just three days before his 36th birthday, and died. They had been together for eight years, and my granddaughter was devastated. Once again we were unable to comfort her or hug her and we are so very close. It was such a bleak, horrendous time. We couldn't go to the funeral as neither of us had had the vaccine, so we had to watch on Zoom, which was heartbreaking. Again, Covid had deprived us of being with our family when we should have been there. My granddaughter is still suffering and does not want to talk very much, so I feel that as well as losing Steve I have almost lost her as well.

2021 also has its milestones: our eldest daughter is 60 in February and our youngest 50 in April, our youngest grandson enters his teens in June, but all celebrations are on hold. We are stuck at home, getting older every day. Time is running out for us. I am so angry about so many things, but it is so much worse for our grandsons. They haven't been to school for almost a year; how will this affect their future? And what will it do to all the young people at university, stuck in their rooms, running up huge bills, hardly learning anything and certainly not being able to enjoy all the fun they should be having? It is too devastating to think about.

I have always been a busy, active person and I have had to put my life on hold. I know there are many millions much worse off than me. But at this stage in my life I should be able to see my grandchildren, meet friends and enjoy going out together. Instead, I look after the house, read, cook, have the weekly shop delivered. Please let it be over by the summer, so that we can enjoy the years that we and everyone else of our age has left. This time will certainly go down in history, but I for one would rather not have been one of the statistics that lived through this dreadful pandemic.

Nineteen

17

Questions

What is the name of the new infectious corona virus disease which led to a world pandemic in 2020?

(ANSWERS IN BACK OF BOOK)

Sarah's story

Phew! What on earth just happened?

Sat here, looking back on the past year, I am not sure how I've managed it. It has been extremely difficult. It has for a lot of people.

Not long before the pandemic I lost my brother Ashley, who was only 58, and suddenly I was one of four siblings instead of one of five. I remember taking on the role as Chief Supporter and organiser for the family. I kept going. Then, when we were a week into the pandemic, my father who was in his early 80s went into hospital, contracted Covid while he was there and died. Fortunately, we were all allowed to see him. We told him we loved him and that he was allowed to leave us now if he wanted. I told him I would look after everyone and my brother was waiting for him, for a cold beer on the 'other side'. Ashley and dad LOVED their beer! It didn't even occur to me at the time to be scared of getting infected; I've always been rather fearless. But it was another immense loss, within weeks of the first one. I kept going.

We were in lockdown and my mother was alone in the house needing support. So I did what I felt I needed to do: I parked a mobile home on my mother's driveway, and went to live in it, so that we could meet up in the garden, have meals together and talk about dad. I am also not embarrassed to admit we drank a lot of rosé. This was around the time we all started clapping the NHS on Thursday evenings. Remember that? I remember clapping as I cried thinking how grateful I was that some gorgeous NHS soul was there holding my dad's hand as he 'slipped into the next room'... Thank you.

During May, in the midst of the pandemic, I had started a new job with Formula E, World Championship. I met all my colleagues via a laptop, virtually, from my living room! There are a lot of younger people in the business who are used to travelling with our race calendar, but Covid put a stop to that. Suddenly, they couldn't go anywhere. Many of them were in shared houses or very small London apartments. As the Chief People Officer people tend to look to me to support them, solve problems and answer questions, some of which there were no answers to. We have all been dealing with a time of ambiguity, fear, risk, loss and uncertainty. As Chief People Officer, you smile, keep optimism flowing, show empathy, patience and strength even when deep down you may yourself be on reserves. Looking back, I realise that I have spent the last year looking after so many people, always carrying on and never stopping to catch my breath. I sometimes felt bombarded with problems, for which people were expecting me to find the solutions. Make it better for them in some way.

If I had been told at the beginning of the pandemic what I could expect over the coming 12 months, I don't think a) I would have believed them; and b) I would have been able to get my head around how I would manage. But when you are in the throes of it, you just do it. You just keep things moving. I guess I subconsciously break things into chunks and tackle them one by one. I've always been very solution-focused. I see a problem and think: 'How do we fix this?' That is quite a common trait in women, we are fixers. Failure has never been an option. I am a lot like my father: an optimist, always in high spirits, entertaining and making it better. What people don't see is that this extroversion is combined with a huge need for introversion and space. But how do you tell people that you need time for yourself, without letting them down? So you don't say anything and sometimes this takes it toll. It usually hits my weak health spot, like a giant warning beacon! I have a chronic condition, Ulcerative Colitis, which was gradually getting worse as 2020 progressed. Having not responded to my meds, I found myself in hospital... masked up with a drip in my arm!! That made me stop briefly... I bloody LOVE the NHS! We must protect it!

Over the past year, I have seen people become more loving, more helpful, with fuller hearts. Conversely, I have seen people who have become more selfish, angrier, and some even take advantage of misfortunes. It's as if every human characteristic has been magnified through this pandemic. I'm sure I'm not the only one who feels like this; many people have had to take on the worries of others and the care for other people. I do think the pandemic has been – and is – extremely hard for women. In the main, they are the carers, the ones who have picked up the pencil and begun home schooling. We know statistically women, other underrepresented groups, and those in poverty are the ones with the most job losses, the most furloughs and highest number of COVID cases.

This will undoubtedly impact their future as well as potentially undo so much of the progress we have made.

There are some great things the pandemic has given us. For me, I have been surrounded by fabulous people, friends and family and a glorious husband, like the brightest of stars in the darkest of nights. We have all heard people talk of the money and time they have saved on those long, wasted commutes to the office.

I don't believe that forced change becomes permanent as a rule, but I do hope some seeds of positive change have been sown. That some have learned to love a little harder and tolerate a little more.

So now, coming through the other side of COVID World... As I queued for my vaccine, the tears were streaming down my face. No idea why. Maybe it's because it was the end of an era. Maybe it's because the vaccine could have saved my father. Maybe I know that my brother would not have been able to cope with the fear and impact of a pandemic.

Or maybe I'm grateful and consider myself lucky. It's probably all of that.

There have been so many changes in our lives, so much going on and we need to find a new way of working through it. I feel the anxiety that so many of us talk about; the lack of confidence that I can't really pinpoint to anything specific.

Life is short and very precious.

I now need to stop, Be still.

Take time to think.

To mourn.

To fix myself a little.

And to take stock...

Phew! What on earth just happened?

Sarah B x

Walking in gratitude

Nothing terrible has happened to me. Nothing to upset the new regularity of my daily life, even in lockdown, but the world has been shaking and groaning in agony all around me. And the enormity of the unfolding tragedy creeps into everything. It creeps closer as those closest to me, but physically not close enough, are impacted on every level.

The anxiety and disbelief caused by the pandemic's ruthless, reckless, destructive course through so many lives, is sometimes hard to manage.

But I am one of the millions who are privileged to be able to just walk. There were the driveway walks when I was locked down abroad waiting for repatriation, the driveway walks in two periods of quarantine and then the longer grateful walks once the gates opened to a slightly wider horizon.

I look closely at every tiny living thing and it all sustains and surprises me. Walking in confined spaces heightens my awareness of the miracles that unfold every day in gardens and hedges and cracks in paving stones.

Putting one foot in front of the other is a gift that is denied now to so many. Walking, thinking, looking and seeing, honouring those lost and those who have given so much...

I have so much to be grateful for.

In dedication

To all those wonderful and dedicated carers who supported vulnerable people at home throughout the lockdowns. We couldn't have managed without you.

SMB

Wet and windy outdoor eating

Wet and windy outside meeting with Wendy Hill and her daughter, Jacqui Ayles

Missing

Annie's story

In the past year, a year that seemed to come straight out of a science fiction film, so many people have been unable to see their grown-up children. Because they had to self-isolate, or because they couldn't travel from one tier to another, or because those children were not part of their bubble. It felt weird, and sad, and difficult. I myself tried to be cool about it, saying that it was easier for me, because my son has been living in Japan for the last ten years. I'm used to it, I said. I said it, but I lied. You never get used to a child who lives far away. Not in COVID times, not at Christmas, not on birthdays and not on everyday days, when you want to have coffee together, or ask him for help because the internet is playing up.

The day he left is still in my heart and my head and in my fingers. I remember what his hair felt like then, and his shoulders in his thin jacket. We took him to the airport in the pouring rain, and when he went through customs, I wanted to shout: 'Don't go!' But you don't say that, as a mother, because you want your child to be happy and if that happiness happens to be in Japan, so be it.

Since then, I've seen him almost every year. I've been to Japan, with my husband and alone. I never went for too long, because ten days are enough for a son when your mother sleeps in your living room on a futon. He has been home a couple of times, and we have met up with him and his Japanese wife in various countries, for a holiday together. It was never enough, but it was good.

This year, there was nothing. The summer holidays were postponed, then the Christmas holidays. Then we stopped making plans. Better luck next year, we said.

But it's tough. Of course, there is Skype, and Skype is much better than nothing, but it's so contrived. You need to talk for at least an hour, otherwise it's not worth it, and the questions you really want to ask, you don't ask. Are you happy? Why do you always cut your hair so short? Are you eating enough? ARE YOU HEALTHY? You talk about other things, and when you say goodbye, you feel empty.

I will never forget the time I saw him on Skype when he moved his body awkwardly, and didn't want to tell me why. In the end, he had to confess that he had had a motorbike accident and spent three days in hospital with a broken collarbone. He'd had a lucky escape, because his motorbike was a write-off. He hadn't wanted to tell me because he knew for sure that I would have taken the first plane there. And he was right, I would have done. I had nightmares for at least a week after that.

And now, there is COVID. My son is head of the English department at a college, and he teaches from home at the moment, and sometimes in class. Talking to him, you would think that there is no such thing as COVID anywhere near him. The shops are open and people can still eat out. Okay, they wear masks, but for Japan, that's not unusual. He and his wife take buses and undergrounds, he goes out with friends, and he says he is healthy. But would he even tell me if he wasn't, and what would I do then, if I can't even take a plane out there?

People say: he'll come back one day. But I don't think so. He has a good life there, and he loves Japan. If he doesn't want to come back – and he doesn't – I don't even want him here. As long as he's happy, and healthy. But I miss the normality of a son close by, the small simple things. Going into town and saying: I'll buy you that jacket. Having a fight, and making up; you don't have fights from a distance. And most of all, in these times, simply being able to feel his forehead and to know: he's fine. He's healthy.

Every day when I wake up, I look at my mobile to see if there's a message from him. Simply to know that he's okay, COVID-free, and all in one piece, because he has a new motorbike by now. When there is a message, my day feels better. But I'll never get used to it, having a faraway child. And I can't wait until the day when the COVID nightmare is over, when the borders are open and we can see each other again. Here, or in Japan, or somewhere in between. Mask-free and worry-free. Apart from that motorbike, of course.

A mixed blessing

Having a baby in Covid times is a unique experience – and to me, in a way, it was a mixed blessing. There are the things you miss, of course, both at the birth and afterwards when you are back home with your baby. No normal baby shower, no pregnancy photo-shoot at the studio, none of the normal things that make pregnancy extra special.

And then, when the baby has arrived, you can't see your family and friends, you can't go to baby groups and social life is non-existent. But there are also good sides, and you learn to improvise. We asked a photographer to come to us and she took pregnancy photos on our doorstep, and other ones once the baby was born. And a socially distanced baby shower is also fun. But best of all: we had precious family time that we never could have had if it wasn't for Covid.

My partner Lewis is a probation officer and I'm a midwife. Once Covid started, we both worked from home most of the time. When Lewis had Zoom meetings or phone interviews, I worked in my own room. Once the baby was born, I went on lots of walks with him, so that when Lewis took part in a court hearing, there would be no baby crying in the background.

As a midwife, I wasn't worried about the birth itself, but I did worry that because of Covid, Lewis wouldn't be able to visit the ward if I had to stay in hospital. I wanted to be in and out as quickly as possible; I didn't even want an epidural in case it slowed things down. But it all went well. My waters broke at home, but I wasn't in labour yet, so the next day Lewis could come to the hospital with me. I went in at 7 a.m. and at 9 p.m. I was at home in bed, with the baby and a Big Mac. The birth itself was a happy experience; we were incredibly well looked after.

Of course, Covid did change things. We didn't quite know what the rules were for visitors at the time, so when the family came to meet baby Toby, we asked them to wear masks. In their first photos with the baby, they all have their faces covered, but looking back, it will be an interesting sign of the time.

Now I'm on maternity leave, and the wonderful thing is that Lewis has been around to witness every step of our son's progress. He was there for the big milestones, for instance when he started crawling, and whenever we had a difficult night we could share the burden. It made it a very special time for both of us.

Toby is nine months old now and last week Lewis went back to two days a week at work. He finds it hard to be away from us, so I send him lots of photos and tell him what's happening at home. He misses spending so much time with Toby.

Covid is still here, but there is light at the end of the tunnel. When my son grows up, he will realise that he was born in a year that was different from all others. During my pregnancy I took loads of photos related to Covid, and put them in a special book. One day, when he's old enough, I will be able to show what it was like, in that year where so many lives ended, and his life began.

Covid-19: A child's view

HOW DID YOU CELEBRATE YOUR BIRTHDAY?

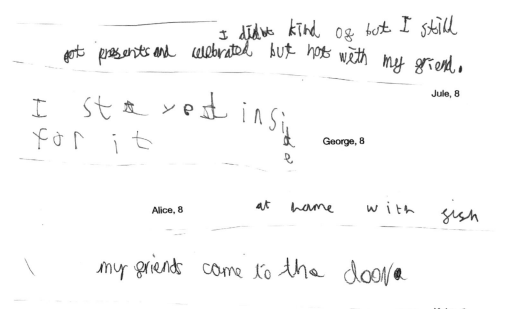

I got presents and celebrated but not with my friend. I didnt kind of but I still

Jule, 8

I stayed insied for it

George, 8

Alice, 8

at home with fish

my friends came to the door

Kuba, 8

Out of category

What a strange feeling this is, basking in the sunshine in my garden in March 2021 and thinking back over the past year. My memory is hazy; I wonder if I'm in denial about the challenges I've faced?

My Covid-19 experience has been defined by my being classified as 'C.E.V.' - clinically extremely vulnerable. It started with an urgent text message on behalf of the NHS telling me to shield; to stay indoors at all costs and to keep all the windows firmly closed. Oh the irony, 12 months on!

A barrage of texts and letters ensued, each more alarming than the last. There was a call from my local council to make sure I was safe (and doing as I was told I suspect) and the weekly delivery of a food parcel. The box contained 'enough food for one person for a week', represented by a bag of potatoes, a loaf of white bread, tinned fruit, baked beans, a bag of apples, tinned meatballs, tinned tomatoes, toilet roll and a couple of hotel size shower gels and shampoo. Sometimes they threw in a bag of pasta; sometimes there were oranges. The box was left at the front door religiously every week until I felt too guilty about accepting it and eventually cancelled it. I had offered it to our local Food bank, only to be told of the dozens of others doing the same and they couldn't take any more supplies.

The point is that I was, and still am, a fit and healthy woman in her mid-fifties. I spend all my time outdoors and being in lockdown, quite literally, was messing with my head. So, rightly or wrongly, I ignored those very disturbing and dramatic text messages and continued to open my windows and to walk my dog. I got used to doing the 'pavement dance' and the 'head twist', the one where you made brief eye contact before swivelling your head to avoid potential Covid germs flying through the air. I walked down the middle of the road to avoid anyone and everyone – the streets were often eerily quiet.

I just felt that it was important to continue doing the small things that gave shape to my day, provided I was careful and considerate. It caused no end of arguments with my husband, aka Captain Covid, as he struggled to restrain me and 'keep me safe'. As if with his overly protective arms around me, Covid would choose not to pick a fight with him. Thankfully, it didn't.

And the months went on. The letters signed by my friend Matt Hancock arrived, only to be shredded and recycled. What a waste of paper. I would love to know how many others like me fell into this category, by dint of some childhood accident like mine.

Amanda Armstrong

But then news of the vaccine arrived. A depressing and lonely Christmas, with last-minute plans to have our kids visit cancelled by our bumbling PM, was marginally improved by the knowledge of the pending jab. And suddenly I was grateful to be in Category 4; there was a light at the end of this very dark tunnel. The tunnel that has seen so much grief and sadness; so much hardship and challenge for so many.

It was unexpectedly emotional, turning up at my GP Surgery and having my vaccination. As if months of ups and downs, highs and lows, were all dissipated by that quick jab in my arm. The thought of seeing and hugging my son, of spending time arguing with my parents over nonsensical banalities, of laughing with friends, of travelling overseas to see my sister and my best friend – these became a reality. So as I wait patiently for my second jab, I reflect on the strangest year, not just for me, but for literally everyone the world over. What a collective experience to be recorded in the annals of history.

Amanda Armstrong (April 2021)

A teacher's tale

We were a lovely class of 30 7 year olds who in September 2019 had taken the giant step of leaving a cosy infant school and started life in a large bustling junior school. Fast forward to March 2020, where with very little warning, our school was disbanded and sent home on that Friday. As their class teacher, I never thought for one moment that we would not be a class together again.

Yes, there were tears as the children walked through the gates to go home. On this Friday when the bell signalled the end of the day, an eerie quiet pervaded the corridors because nobody really understood what was happening. A far cry from the delighted yells and shrieks of a normal Friday home time with the playground crammed with parents chatting as their children kicked footballs or climbed over apparatus planning their weekend. Oh no, this Friday was different. For the first time ever, children were not excited that it was the end of a school week. Their exit was hushed and the playground for once stood empty as anxious parents collected their children and made a hasty retreat, not knowing when their child would return.

And so began 'Lockdown' schooling.

Small classes of 15 children in the first lockdown. Between the endless hand washing and sanitising I think we achieved some learning....At least I hope we did. The hand washing took some getting used to, particularly with seven year olds, whose arms could barely reach over the classroom sink to reach the water tap. It was of course a precise military operation to ensure 30 hands were washed on entering the classroom, exiting the classroom, before play after play, before lunch, as they left for lunch play, re-entering the classroom and before they left to go home. Many hands, including mine became red, sore and stung when hand gel was administered. But we did it and made up many ways of making it fun.....

Playtimes were interesting. Each class had an area to play in, luckily it was summer term and we had a lovely field to divide up. Playtimes were staggered and classes could only play with whoever was in their class. No mixing of brothers, sisters or friends in other classes or year groups. When I think back now, I realise how accepting and resilient our pupils were. How hard it must have been for them to not have their special friends to play with.

PE & Games was a challenge. Our ruling was not to share equipment. So a simple game of rounders or cricket became an operational nightmare:

1.   All hands sanitised as they ran out to the field.

2.   All balls, bats in fact ANY equipment was doused in Milton sterilising fluid at the beginning of the lesson, while the class ran around the track.

3.   A game was finally enjoyed.....However a careful eye had to be kept on the clock to ensure ample time to sterilise ALL equipment that had been touched by human hands....As well as the relentless act of hand washing upon entering the classroom.....Only to have to wash them again before they went home.

But we did it. The children at school were happy. For the children and parents at home every day it was tough. The parents all did their part in home educating and from what I witnessed it was a far harder job We said goodbye to our Lockdown classes in July and welcomed a new, eager class of 30 through the gates in September. And no, I didn't for one moment think it would all happen again. But it did.

Monday January 4th 2021 we returned as a class to school for one day.

Tuesday January 5th Schools were now closed for the majority of pupils. My lovely class were once again no more.

This time Google Classroom dominated. I have been teaching for over 30 years and this new lockdown meant my "techy" skills would be severely stretched and yes, they were. For parents it was a far better medium for daily lessons. It also allowed us to meet as a class every day. So, the children in my class who were at home logged on and could see me and the rest of the class. This time it was the constant reminder to, "please mute, we can hear you at home." What this really meant was the entire class could hear whatever the rest of the family was up to. I have to admit, I have a few amusing stories of non-muters but that is for another time.

This time we had "bubble" classes. Two classes merged together with no more than 28 pupils. One teacher taught "live" children, the other taught remotely. We swapped each day. The inexorable hand washing ensued. January and February are not ideal months to be in Lockdown at school with strict social distancing rules. Wet playtimes and lunchtimes where children were not permitted to move places or move around were excruciatingly difficult. I decided painting on one particularly wet afternoon would be a wonderful mindful activity. Oh how wrong I was. In theory, it should have been a marvellously creative afternoon with soothing background music. In reality it was my lunchtime spent sanitising paint brushes, water pots and paint palettes. In an attempt to avoid 28 children converging at the sink to change murky water, I spent the entire lesson traipsing around changing water for them and being rather irritable when requests were made to change paintbrushes. After school was spent sanitising paint brushes, paint palettes and water pots. It had seemed such a good idea after they had been cooped up all day ....

March 8th arrived and we became a class again. Well, for one day at least as the very next day, our class had a positive case and the half of my class that had been in school over Lockdown were sent home to isolate.

I have many memories of this Lockdown. The true heroes are all you mums, dads, grans and grandads who embraced the home learning; Who shared laptops so that your children had access to education; Who juggled parenting with teaching and doing your job at the same time.

You were amazing. As were all the children who have had to adapt to so many challenges the world has not seen before.

To end on a positive, Lockdown seems to have fostered resilience, creativity and team work amongst children.

My thoughts go out to everyone who has lost somebody dear to them during this time.

Teacher for 34 years

The year of the plague

2020 – Throughout history there have always been 'plagues'. To me, this was another in the 21st century and I have therefore named it so. This is our story of how we approached living through the challenges, my husband Trevor and I. We are lucky enough to live in the countryside and have been blessed to have plenty of space around us during this year. I am known locally as 'the mad hatter' as I am mostly seen wearing some form of head covering.

My best memory is of the sense of community. Trevor and I are over 70 and fit however we had immediate offers of help with our shopping, The local egg barn expanded their entrepreneurial skills and launched a village shop in a summer house. This has been a lifesaver for essentials like milk and bread.

Another memory is the wonderful weather that allowed us to spend a lot of time outdoors. June is a special month for us, our wedding anniversary and my birthday so a great chance to dress up and celebrate in style.

No yoga in classes, but in the garden every Friday morning and our yoga bubble of 6 was able to continue this until September. No swimming at the leisure centre pool, but July saw us making a pilgrimage to the coast and braving the sea. We were able to repeat this three more times over the summer. No dinners out, but organising meals at home for two has become a dominant feature of lockdown for sure.

There were still opportunities presenting themselves to use themes to dress up and dress for dinner. We enjoyed paying tribute to Honor Blackman when she died and we did 007 as a dressing up theme.

The New Year brought snow and time to throw on some clothes and do a photoshoot to make this another fun occasion,

I vowed to capture the year of the plague in pictures and kicked off this resolve on 8 March 2020. My philosophy is that there is always something to look forward to whilst "'living in the moment". Doing what is possible during lockdown cements ones own purpose to keep moving forward towards normality again. I count my blessings having a loving husband to share life with and all its ups and downs. The resolve made early was to concentrate on what we could do as opposed to what we could not.

Monica

Ready for the outside world

007 and Pussy Galore eat your heart out

Local enterprise village shop opened in lockdown

Birthday celebrations

Yoga on the lawn. Ouch it's hurting!

White witch of Halloween

Happiness by the sea. All aglow

Snowing in Dorset

This can't be happening!

Christmas for two. Festive greetings

Helping the homeless during covid

Having volunteered at a local charity shop for over 20 years, it came as a great shock to have to close up indefinitely in February 2020 due to Covid-19.

I'm no good at sewing. Whilst a lot of my friends and family got involved with making scrub bags, face masks and the like, like many others, I suddenly had a lot of time on my hands. I looked for an alternative way to help others in need via a friend of mine who has links with rehoming homeless people and the local women's refuge.

I got my address book out and gradually contacted all my local friends and family to let them know that, even though charity shops were shut for the foreseeable future, if they were having a clear out, I could help move on their unwanted clothes, bedding, kitchenalia, electrical goods, cutlery, china and bric a brac.

Of course, everybody else was in the same boat - lots of time on their hands, tidying up their homes, having a spring clean, but as all the charity shops and tips were closed, they had nowhere to take their unwanted stuff.

The Chalet

As you can imagine I had an absolutely overwhelming response - it even went viral on several local roads near my home who set up their own street WhatsApp groups, so the word quickly spread.

Luckily we've got a chalet in the garden which quickly became filled to the rafters and gradually, in time, my friend and I were able to donate whatever was needed. It was especially satisfying when the charity, Pivotal Outreach, was able to purchase a property, pluck somebody off the streets and set them up in their own home.

Similarly the local women's refuge were very grateful for ladies' and childrens' clothing along with toiletries and other items.

There are some extremely generous and kind people out there. People who want to get involved in whatever way they can to help somebody less fortunate than themselves and, it was very heart warming to know that it was a win-win situation for everyone,

Would I do it again? Yes, most definitely but I was extremely fortunate to have a very understanding and patient husband who helped me throughout - thank you Mr W!

In dedication

To be thankful I have Vivienne as a mother in law is an understatement, always there with advice, encouragement, energy and joy. Her achievement with her fulfilled projects through this difficult time is truly inspiring and amazing as she has been throughout her life, we are so proud of her.

Lydia Lee

Dogs in lockdown

Flora - Long Haired Dachshund

Walter - Cockapoo

Cosmic - Frenchton

Bear - Bernedoodle

Honky - Jack Russell

Lucy - Flat Coated Retriever

Sybil - Parti Poodle

Otis - Working Cocker Spaniel

Being a medical student in covid times

"For the first time I called my mum and cried"

I was in the middle of my third year of a medical degree in March 2020 when Covid hit. At that point we were doing blocks of practice in hospital to gain experience in all aspects of medicine. My university and training hospital are in the Midlands, a hotbed for Covid in that initial wave. We all desperately wanted to be involved and help in the hospitals that were fast filling up. However, as we were only in our third year we were told to pack our bags and go home, to complete virtual studies and offer help where we could near home. In other words: "You'll be in the way if you all stay here!"

So I spent the spring and summer of 2020 in lockdown with my family, doing some studying, working in a school for vulnerable children and spending a lot of my time walking and sunning myself. To be honest, I loved it!

In September the number of Covid cases had eased and we were able to return to university and the hospital to continue our training. We had all missed blocks of practice, but as most of them are repeated, it seemed that we would be able to catch up and no harm had been done to our training. So back we all went to our hospitals and clinical practices, self-testing regularly.

As the weeks went by, the number of cases started to rise again and this soon became evident in the hospital I was working in. Before we knew it, Covid cases were back up to dangerous levels. On one particular day I went in to start my shift on a Renal ward. One of the men on the ward was coughing persistently. We were able to put him in a separate room and quickly administer a Covid test to him and the other patients on the ward. As the results started to come back, we put any patients testing positive in separate rooms. However, it soon became apparent that we had run out of individual rooms and there were more positive cases than negative.

Therefore we changed the status of the ward and the shift that had started on a Renal ward finished on a Covid ward! I returned home to my digs that night deflated, upset and very anxious.

Apart from the worry about the worsening situation in the hospitals, we as medical students were also concerned whether we would have the opportunity to gain the range of experience necessary to pass our qualifications and become doctors. As the hospitals became overrun with Covid patients, fewer people were being admitted to hospital with other conditions and for other planned treatments and operations. We were having a very different experience to the students in the preceding years. Because there were very few patients having non-essential procedures, there was little hope of us seeing, for example, a hip replacement. The Junior Doctors were largely required to work in Intensive Care and we were doing much of the work of the Junior Doctors on the wards. It was both exhilarating and terrifying.

As the days passed, our training had to be adapted to the situation. We were required to complete our blocks of practice, as well as work days on the Infectious Diseases ward, which had, of course, become exclusively Covid wards. Up until this point, I had prided myself on being strong and felt that I never became too emotionally involved when things got difficult. But on one particular day I crumpled.

We had lost two patients to Covid on my ward in the morning and as I walked home for my lunch break I knew that a third person would be gone by the time I returned for the afternoon. It was so desperately sad, yet it was somehow a privilege to be with these people, to hold their hands and take the place of their loved ones at the end of their lives.

For the first time I phoned my mum and cried. This was a particularly harrowing day that took its toll on all the doctors and nurses on the ward. At the end of the shift the consultant kindly told me that he too had found it tough. He suggested that I go home and pour myself a large glass of wine, just as he would be doing.

We all suffered, but none more so than the patients who lost the battle and their families who couldn't be with them.

The lessons that were never learned

School closures: I don't think any of us really believed it until we heard it on that Wednesday evening. The two days after the announcement were a blur as we continued to teach the children in school, whilst reassuring them that things would all work out. We started preparing Home Learning Packs for children to take home on Friday; adapting and changing all the existing planning to ensure it was accessible to all, whether in school or out. Senior Leaders were racing around trying to ascertain which pupils were likely to still be in school - vulnerable children or children of key workers - from Monday so they could be arranged in bubbles. The very logistics of accommodating so many children in so few rooms involved a huge migration of desks, seats and equipment to maintain social distancing. At that point, the world and his dog were claiming they were key workers and it was looking as if almost half the school would be in. Thankfully as the weekend approached and with the government clarifying who classified as key workers, many made the decision to keep their children at home.

Over the following weeks, the guidelines changed daily for bubbles, self-isolating, inspections and expectations both in school and out. School staff tried to keep up with providing free school meals and work packs for children who weren't attending school. The big failure of the government here was not to realise that although our most vulnerable children were entitled to attend school, they are also vulnerable for a reason: they were the least likely to arrive even on a good day. I worried for so many pupils in my class as I know their home lives were often less than ideal. The pastoral team did an amazing job during lockdown; dealing with numerous safeguarding incidents, keeping in touch with parents and children and trying to make sure everyone had access to some kind of provision.

In the end, there were children we did not see for six months. I'm not sure we'll ever really know the impact those six months of not just missed education but missed socialisation will have had on their mental health and wellbeing. I do know that we lost these children for a while. And that despite there being a huge push from schools to ensure health and wellbeing was on the agenda when the children returned, no one really knew what that looked like. Social services were overwhelmed and as educators, we were expected to pick up the slack and find time in a six- hour school day to address six months of missed learning, bereavement, re-socialisation, hand-washing and mental well-being. No one ever provided the extra hours a day we would need to do that. Nor the training. The idea that adding after-school classes, weekend school and holiday clubs would fill these gaps was laughable. Anyone picking up their child at the end of the day will know how saturated their brains are already. How exhausted they are by the end of a half term, never mind term.

It wasn't all doom and gloom though. In many ways it became the teaching job of my dreams! Being at school was the best of it. At the beginning of June, when some year groups returned, I had a class of 12 key worker children: a mix of year groups, mixed ability and children who were excited to be back at school. Due to the low numbers and the summer sky we were able to do the kind of child-led teaching I had always wanted to do. I had the time to listen properly to every child reading every day. I could give each child some individual tuition and time – something that's so difficult with a class of 30. We were able to explore the things that the children found interesting, experiment with new ways of delivering learning, venture outside to use the outdoor areas and do more practical activities; things that are too difficult to manage with a typical ratio of 1:30. We found a real joy in reading together as a class for an extended period every day and discussing topics we wouldn't normally have time for in a packed curriculum timetable. These were all the best parts of the job!

All of this made the return in September all the more painful. To realise that all the government was interested in was 'catching-up' the children. Squeezing 6 months of missed learning into the autumn term. Ignoring the fact that adjusting back to a full day was a huge feat for many. That there was a huge disparity between the children who had parents who supported home-learning for six months and those who were left to fend for themselves, between those who had equipment at home to learn online and those who had been borrowing a parent's phone for a few minutes at a time to do some work - and those who had nothing. I think I felt so let down that the lessons we could have learned from that change to the exam routine (I have four children of my own, including one who was spared Year 6 SATS and one in her GCSE year) were instantly forgotten on return to school. The moments of respect earned by school staff early on in the pandemic for sorting out a whole new teaching curriculum and adapting to online learning in a matter of days, as well as any appreciation for the fact that educating nowadays is so much more than teaching the 3 Rs, was so quickly forgotten and replaced by the typical politicisation of the sector. It made me sad and disappointed that the narrative continued to be that schools had been shut.

I feel privileged to have been a part of the school team during the pandemic, but I have now left teaching. If a pandemic couldn't change the way we approach the education of children in this country, nothing will.

Covid-19: A child's view

WHAT ADVICE WOULD YOU GIVE TO THE LEADERS OF THE COUNTRY?

allow children to speak there thoughs

Tilly, 8

Berna, 7

To stop the virus

don't do another lockdown..

Arthur 8

This is advice for India.
I think you should get
some more oxygen tanks.

Ollie ,6

I'll help you.

Jeremiah, 8

To not keep us away from our friends

Kuba, 8

The new mother

My baby's eyes are too wide. They glisten and stare.
I hardly know what I'll find in there.
Staring back is my own reflection,
One of fear and sorrow - not perfection.
I pray for days that are sunnier to approach,
But anxiety makes me full of reproach,
Will I or my loved ones still be here?
To dance with her under skies clear?
Or will there be a cloud of sorrow
That hangs like fog on my child's furrow?
To miss a moment those eyes might see
To be taken from all that her future might be
Is a fear that has more grounding than before
This - my baby, the one I adore
Has changed everything; the ground has shifted
In a moment I can be uplifted
Then come crashing down as the news unfurls
I pray that my baby will grow up in a better world.

Nineteen

18

Questions

What is the name for the level of restrictions in a given area of the country at certain times, based on the severity of the spread of the disease?

(ANSWERS IN BACK OF BOOK)

A Covid Playlist

We'll Meet Again
Vera Lynn

What's Going On
Marvin Gaye

Ain't No Mountain High Enough
Marvin Gaye & Tammi Terrell

Toxic
Britney Spears

Let's Stay Together
Al Green

Breathe
Blu Cantrell, Sean Paul

All By Myself
Jamie O'Neal

Shackles
Mary Mary

That's Life
Frank Sinatra

Don't Dream It's Over
Crowded House

Don't Stand So Close To Me
Police

I'm Still Standing
Elton John

Life's What You Make It
Talk Talk

People Help The People
Birdy

Love's In Need of Love Today
Stevie Wonder

The Prayer
Celine Dion & Andrea Bocelli

Get Here
Oleta Adams

Human
Rag'n'Bone Man

If The World Was Ending
JP Saxe & Julia Micaels

Mask Off
Future

Hands To Myself
Selina Gomez

Times Like These
Foo Fighters & Live Lounge All Stars

I Will Survive
Gloria Gaynor

Bury A Friend
Billie Eillish

We Were Raised Under Grey Skies
JP Cooper

Where Is The Love
Black Eyed Peas

The Sound of Silence
Disturbed

Outside
George Michael

A Million Years Ago
Adele

Bills
Lunch Money Lewis

I Need A Dollar
Alloe Blacc

Zoom
Fat Larry's Band

Marea (We've Lost Dancing)
Fred again.. & The Blessed Madonna

When Will I See You Again
The Three Degrees

ADD SONG TITLES WHICH HAVE HELD MEANING FOR YOU DURING 2020

1. _____

2. _____

3. _____

4. _____

5. _____

Apocalypse snow

I decided to tick one off the bucket list and take a ski instructor course. Did I want to become a ski instructor? Not really. I just thought it would be cool to be professionally taught to be a better skier for six weeks in the mountains of Whistler, Canada. It also sounded great to be on a course with 50 other people and to live with nine others in a huge house that happened to have a hot tub, in a village known for its partying. I had wanted to do a ski season since I was 18.... And since I was now 27, I thought it was about time. The house we lived in was called the Snow Goose. Later on in the year I got a tattoo of a goose with skis and a stupid hat on my ankle, because this house meant a lot to me... But I'll get to that later.

November 2019

I was skiing, partying, skiing, more partying and burning through money like a boss. When the ski course finished, I got a random job working as a mobile security alarm responder. Easiest job I have ever done. On top of that, I worked part time as a doorman for two pubs. I have to include that I'm not a scary meathead. You do not have to be big to be a doorman in Whistler. I also worked at a club on Sundays as a videographer. With all these jobs my life was very busy and with all the friends from work plus my ski course buddies, I had an amazing social life. To put things into perspective, I was paying 1550 Canadian dollars a month to live in a private room and I believe I would sleep there an average of seven nights a month. I was having the time of my life.

March 2020

The Mountain shut, followed quickly by all the pubs and restaurants and other businesses. Everyone from my ski course left to go home. Trying to find someone who was staying was getting harder and harder. There were simply no jobs. If you were lucky, there were a few hours' shifts at the one shop that remained open on reduced hours. The mood in the village was not a happy one. People were worried, scared about the virus that was coming and sad at the prospect of leaving a place many of us were calling home. Many of them left so quickly that I didn't get to say goodbye to the majority of my friends. Every day, rows of coaches were taking people away, turning what was once a social Mecca into a ghost town. Yet I was weirdly okay with it. It sucked that everyone was leaving and the situation did cause concern, but the week before, I had met a little ginger German called Louisa, and she made everything else going on seem irrelevant. In fact, my adventure in Whistler had just started.

March 10th 2020

I was working on the door at one of the pubs. This girl walked past me and made a kind of obvious face indicating that she found me attractive and was not afraid to show it. I believe she was quite drunk. She came back later that night and I ended up chatting to her during my whole shift, neglecting my doorman role. There was a strong chance the pub was full of underage drinkers.

We hung out all night, and then the next day and the next. I had met hundreds of girls in Whistler since I arrived there, but with Louisa it was instantly different. She was weird, a free spirit, passionate about animals, deeply kind, philosophical and fun. Living in such a shallow, social media-filled, disingenuous world, finding someone that was so genuine and real made me want to hold on to that. When people started leaving we made a pact to not leave each other.

March 17th 2020

Our first challenge was we didn't have anywhere to stay together. Louisa was sleeping on a sofa in a shared house as she had just moved to Whistler. My flat mates were a couple and they didn't want her coming around due to Covid. Of course everyone was taking the Covid situation seriously and people who stayed there were mostly isolating following the news and government advice. For my security driver job I had to drive around patrolling houses in case alarms were triggered. By then, there was so little going on in and around town that I could walk for hours and not see another soul. But it did mean that Louisa and I had to hang out in car parks or wherever we could meet, and there was nowhere we could stay together. No hotels, no Airbnb – and our own accommodation was off-limits to each other. Then a friend said we could stay in the Snow Goose. The house where I had lived during the training course stood empty because everybody had left. So now we had a six-bedroom house to ourselves with a ridiculous amount of food and alcohol that had been left in everyone's rushed exit. Drinks in the hot tub surrounded by snow, fires in the lounge and walks to the lake - we were apocalypse buddies. It was amazing... until the house manager walked in and found us there.

Rocky Mountains view

April 2020

Shortly after that we moved in together properly; we found a house with like-minded people. We would get drunk and go sledding and have house parties with just us, our bubble of eight. Because there were literally no elderly people in the mountain ski town, it felt like Neverland. In spite of this, I did wonder if I had made the right choice to not go home; I worried about my family there. My work visa was nearly up and so I had the challenge of finding a cash job. Louisa was still trying to find a job herself, and our small amount of money was running out.

July 2020

Summer turned out to be better than winter. I found a cash job installing irrigation and Louisa got a job in a pie shop. The bars and restaurants were open with restrictions. Whistler had come to life again. By now we had a large group of friends. We bought a small rickety camper and would go camping every weekend with friends at different lakes. We rented a boat with a hot tub on it (of course) and had a weekend boat party with 10 of us. Louisa and I went on a road trip to Vancouver Island and to the cool and beautiful surf town of Tofino. By now we were even more smitten with each other.

the perimeter of the 'hotel grounds' he spots some workmen clearing out a large pond. They've removed some fence panels to allow access for a digger. Dad shows great interest in this activity, chats away merrily and then disappears through the hole in the fence - only to be caught, brought back and reported.

To help me avoid a 150-mile round trip to support my family during this time, a dear friend offers me the use of his mother's empty and ancient cottage in a pretty Surrey village so that I can buzz between sister and dad with ease. The visits to dad are 'through the window pane' and the visits to sister consist of a walk across summer Surrey fields together.

At the end of the day I sit in the cottage's sunny garden in the summer evening light, listening to birdsong, glass of wine in hand, wondering how on earth things would have sorted themselves if it wasn't for furlough and the kindness of strangers, friends and charity. Without these we wouldn't have been able to help my sister. It was Covid that created the catalyst for her to make change.

The outcome of this situation is good. My sister and brother-in-law seek counselling and return to married life, happier than they have been for years. Dad is back in his home – healthy, vaccinated and happy - and my husband Bill is able to watch Naked Attraction at the right volume.

Covid Botanical illustration
by Jenny Malcolm

Freedom in lockdown

I suppose you could say I'm a country girl. I was brought up around farms and have always had a love of animals and the countryside. I have a total fascination for nature and, growing up where I did, helped my curiosity blossom. It was inevitable that being around nature and horses was going to be my intended destiny ..... much to my long suffering mother's disapproval.

My husband John, shared my passion for horses and supported my career as a western riding instructor. We lived in the country but, in recent years had found that the market town where we lived was changing significantly. 500 new homes had been built around us and there are plans for another 500 in the coming years. The countryside I loved so much was changing before my eyes.

In the UK there are approximately 3,000 quarter horses compared with 30,000 in Germany where they also have their own Western Riding Association, rivalling that of the USA. John and I realised that if I wanted to progress within my career and continue to live in a rural location, we would need to make a life-changing move to Germany.

Jo and Summer - her dream horse

In 2018 we found our ideal location in North Germany, between Hanover and Hamburg and purchased some land where we intended to build our dream home. John's business was a building company which designed and built log cabins and this 'grand design' would be his last build. We had friends close by who owned a western riding ranch and we planned our perfect life in Lower Saxony.

We had been procrastinating over the actual move date until early 2020 when I finally said that we were going make this move in September come what may! At the time we had no idea what was about to come.

We started putting our plans into action. We had 9 horses but knew that we couldn't take all of them with us so we started the process of rehoming and selling 4 of them. This was not going to be an ordinary house move, with 5 horses, 2 dogs and 2 cats in tow!

Then lockdown hit. The road where our stables were had become very busy and our twice daily trips to the stables involved an awful lot of sitting in traffic. Suddenly, the roads were clear, peace descended and this journey was so much easier.

The large housing development site behind our horse fields was now empty. All the dust and noise ceased - it was silent. There were no planes in the sky and I noticed how different the horses were. I hadn't realised the impact of the noise pollution on them until I noticed how much calmer and happier they were. This strengthened my resolve to get them to the rural and peaceful setting in Germany as soon as possible.

I loved lockdown! Finally some peace and quiet away from the incessant noise we humans make … No more cars, no more building, no more shouting from the builders opposite our fields. And the best thing? I could hear birds sing ….heaven.

There was one downside to lockdown and the imminent move in that I had to let my staff go. I felt so sad letting my lovely team of helpers go. They loved the horses and were reliant on the small income. I felt very bad for them and this was hard for us. I am happy to say that we all still keep in touch though and maybe one day they will be able to visit. After a while, however, I got used to having the place to myself and quite enjoyed it. It was great for John and I to work together with our horses and it gave us time to plan for our epic move.

The weather in the UK during April and May was superb and continued all summer. This enabled me to have a fantastic time riding every day in the sunshine. As any horse owner knows, a large proportion of your life is spent outside on wet and cold days so this summer was a welcome change.

We started to notice the wildlife returning to the area, birds, Badgers, Foxes and Buzzards. One day I even saw a white tailed Eagle. I looked it up and apparently there had been other sightings of this bird which had not been seen in the UK for over 20 years.

These were truly halcyon days and I have beautiful memories of our last weeks in the UK. It was all quite humbling. I realised that as a race, mankind is surplus to requirements. Without us the world would carry on. I hoped we would learn something from this time and realise that we need to treat our planet better.

During the summer I became more of a housewife than ever before, I cooked more and found pleasure in doing so and I even grew our own produce in the garden. Despite having less furniture and belongings, as more and more things were packed away, I embraced the summer of 2020.

By the end of the summer we were out of lockdown and we were set to move on 30 September. Moving the horses was quite straightforward. We had hired a company to transport them and our German contacts owned the ranch where they were going to be when we arrived.

Moving the pets was a different story. They needed passports and vaccinations. I wasn't too worried about the dogs as they were fine in the car and there was a kennel in the overnight ferry. My main worry was Hermione, my Syrian rescue cat who was not a good traveller and she made her displeasure known. As soon as I put her in her crate she pee'd in it and then continued to be vocal and disruptive for the entire journey.

We set off in convoy. I was driving my car and towing a horse trailer. John was driving his car and towing another trailer. Most of our furniture was in a shipping container en route to Germany. We had had to leave some in the stable block for collection at a later date. Part of the way through the drive to Harwich, I had to move Hermione into the the horse trailer as her endless howling was becoming hard to contend with.

We had an overnight crossing and landed in the Hook of Holland at 7am the next morning. Ahead of us was a 10 hour journey. For some reason, known only to John, he decided to take a 'short cut'. We ended up on what has to be described as a cycle path. We went under a bridge and it was only later that I found out the horse trailer was a little too tall for that bridge and all the skylights had been broken. Hermione might have enjoyed a sky view and northern Germany might have enjoyed a Syrian cat screeching as we drove past. I was blissfully unaware.

We had a rental house pre-booked and, actually, we were incredibly lucky with the timing of our move as Germany went into lockdown and closed its borders soon after we arrived. If we hadn't have left in September we may still be trying to get here.

The house that John built

During lockdown, John got to work with the build. Obviously, Covid had some impact on this process. Appointments had to be arranged to view kitchen and bathroom fittings and most things took a lot more organisation and planning. We had a team of Lithuanian builders pre-booked and they needed to have negative covid tests and quarantine for a week before they could come to Germany the first time. They are back now and this time they didn't have to quarantine.

It seems that a lot of Germans are taking staycations and, luckily for us, John had included a self-contained flat as part of the house design. Hopefully this has helped to 'future-proof' our move.

We have now been here for 6 months and are blissfully happy. I am riding every day and feel that the standard of instruction I am receiving and my increased knowledge has made this move worthwhile already. I am looking forward to my first competition in a few weeks' time.

We have both had our vaccinations now as John was in the 'at risk' category and, as his primary carer, I was included in the vaccination programme.

Of course, we really miss friends and most especially, my stepdaughter who we haven't been able to see since September. I hope we can rectify this soon. I am so grateful for FaceTime and Zoom which has made keeping in touch a lot more personal, even during lockdown. I wouldn't say no if Costa ever decided to open up in Germany too.

It may be considered brave to change your life completely in normal circumstances. Even more so to move to a European country during Brexit and in the middle of a global pandemic. We just feel so lucky and I can truly say that we are living our dream life.

Jo Corringham

Nineteen

19

What is the three word slogan for the government advice to limit the spread of a disease?

Questions

(ANSWERS IN BACK OF BOOK)

Covid-19: A child's view

WHAT ARE YOU MOST LOOKING FORWARD TO DOING ONCE YOU ARE ALLOWED?

having
a huge
Party

Jeevan, 8

having a sleep over at my freinds

Josh, 7

life being normal for once

Tilly, 8

being
happy

Isaac, 8

Covid Botanical illustration
by Jenny Malcolm

Cheated, amazed and left speechless

Within the context of this book I find it almost embarrassing to say that, for me, lockdown was an uplifting and amazing experience. Of course the suffering that some had to endure was unimaginable and the sacrifices we were asked to make were hard. However, considering we were (and still are) experiencing a global pandemic, putting one's own wants and priorities aside for the greater good was the least we could do. The strength, resilience and attitude of my family, parents and friends were humbling. A time to be proud of those I hold dear.

Cheated out of a retirement

I retired at the end of 2019 and was looking forward to a life of frequent visits to the coffee shops of Poole with my friends, more time in the sea and carefree walks on the Jurassic Coast, while my family were occupied with school and work. Perfect. Then all of a sudden I had a houseful of people that I had to share my free time with... disaster. Surely they were going to find out about my afternoon nap routine and secret tea and biscuit addiction? This was never the plan. The dog and I were going to have to up our game and start looking busy. On the last day of normality we were sitting in the hammock and looked at each other and knew life was going to change. It did, for the better. We connected again as a family and I was amazed by each of them.

Amazed at my children

First there is my son, Noah aged 16. Two things we had been saying to him for years were stop looking at screens and get out and get some exercise. Of course, we received the expected teenage response. Covid changed this. We then insisted he spent a good part of the day looking at a screen doing schoolwork and to keep in contact with his friends. Where did all the dangers of looking at phones and laptops we had been preaching about for years suddenly disappear to? We didn't discuss this. I think we overlook how hard this time must have been for all the children. We hear a lot about adults and how they had to start working from home, but I think it is many times worse for a child who has to give up school with friends and space to move and instead has to learn to study from home, often with teachers who struggle to get to grips with this new way of schooling as well. Noah did this amazingly well and I respect him for that.

Then there is exercise. If I had asked him to simply get on his bike and come with me for a cycle in the dark and the pouring rain I'm confident this would not have gone down well. But if you add the ingredients of employment and money, this seems to be a far more appealing activity. Noah was desperate, along with a lot of the country, to get a part time job. He found a delivery job. As parents, we were pleased, as it entailed minimal contact with people and he got exercise. So, in the evening he would leave the comfort and warmth of his home and deliver Fish and Chips to the people of Wimborne. He did it, he didn't really complain, but I will never forget his face when he had to leave a plate of lovely food to go outside in the depths of winter. Not his comfort zone.

Winter delivery

My daughter, Paige, is 15. She has also had to deal with the challenges of the new education system, and she, too, has done amazingly well. There is another thing she has done well. Last year I asked Paige to make sure we went to the beach for a swim as much as possible throughout the summer. She took up this request. We had many swims that summer, even on windy, cold English summer days and evenings. These turned into swimming into September, then into October. Every

Monday and Thursday we went to the beach at 6.30 to see what the weather could throw at us. Could we make Paige's birthday in November? Of course we could. The shortest day was then followed by a Christmas day dip, then we went into 2021 and through the Beast from the East 2. February and March came and went and then the coldest start of a year for a long time. It is now the end of May and it is still shocking how cold some mornings are. We are excited to keep going throughout this summer, exploring new to places to take a dip and then get ready for next winter.

To make things clear, this is a 15-year old girl, swimming in freezing conditions (bear in mind that stones were freezing onto our towel on New Year's Eve in Weymouth on our last dip of 2020,) wearing a bikini that is more suitable for Ibiza in mid-summer than a British beach in mid-winter. On schooldays she gets dressed for school on the beach. I would be surprised if there are many if any other 15-year old girls doing this. My only frustration is when people give me credit for getting my daughter to do this. She wants to do this. My respect and thanks go out to Paige for doing it; our trips to the beach have kept me sane and helped me in ways no one will never know.

Sunrise swim

Left speechless by my partner

And then there is my partner. There are many amazing things that she has done during lockdown, such as arranging family Zooms to keep everyone connected (even though the combination of old people and technology meant it was entertaining in a very different way than expected), the Sunday roasts and all the little things I will never know about or notice, but that make a huge difference to a peaceful family life. This alone deserves the ultimate gratitude. Add to this how she adapted to changing her business from a very personal and caring face-to-face experience to an online Zoom affair. The learning curve of technology was immensely steep and reluctantly embraced, she attended numerous online training courses and even passed a further qualification. What was not compromised was her passion for the health and wellbeing of her clients. In fact it was greater than ever, as she knew how important it would be for her clients to have some normality in these crazy times. She also realised that to keep moving and be connected to other people outside your own home was important for both physical and mental health.

But following one sleepless night things got even crazier. She came up with an idea to raise money for charity by bringing people together to share experiences about recent times. Understanding the concept and having witnessed the dedication to this project, I put this venture up there with all other charity events held over the lockdown period, even comparable to the great Sir Tom Moore. Her level of commitment, dedication to detail and determination came as no surprise to anyone who knows her. Anything my partner puts her mind to is done with passion, efficiency and excellence. What I find the most moving part of her journey through this project is that in a way, it started many years ago with the relationships she has formed with her friends. The care and compassion she has given to her clients and friends over the years is second to none. So, when they heard about her amazing idea they were there to help as much as they could. Not from a feeling of duty, but out of a genuine love and connection that has developed over many years. The love and care she has shown to her friends and clients was being repaid and I know she found this very emotional.

I find it hard to express how brilliant I think she is and how much I love her.

"Oh, my partner's name is Yassamin. The project is a book called 19 and 20 and Me"

For Poppy – what happened next

When I wrote the first part of my story, it was an outpouring of my emotions. I have not and cannot read what I wrote that day, but I know that the experience of writing it was cathartic for me and has been invaluable in my recovery from the devastating events of March 2020. I did know that I felt my mother's strength inside me urging me to press on and to be strong and that has only increased as time has passed. I am not the same Beth I was a year ago, people who know me thought I would struggle to survive let alone achieve all that has followed.

Thankfully, my dad and the rest of us recovered from Covid. Dad is 86 and had been with my mum for over 62 years. He has moved into a beautiful new flat and, although it's as tough as hell, he is getting on with his life. When I started to feel a little better, I threw myself into my work, it was what helped me to cope. The knowledge that I was making a difference was my salvation and, even though I work extremely hard, I am passionate about it and my work rejuvenates me.

The ArtsforLifeProject started about 4 years ago. It was an idea between myself and my friend whilst we were dog-walking. Our aim is to help young people with mental health and learning difficulties integrate into the wider community through the therapeutic value of creative arts. My friend and co founder, Jacqui Dennaford, is a psychotherapist and I am an artist. We realised that by working together we could have a far greater impact on the lives of the young people we were trying to support separately. It started in my kitchen. I have three children of my own, Savannah, Cassidy and Luke, who were truly amazing and supportive to me opening up our modest home. By the time we had 60 children a week walking through my door we knew we needed to find premises.

We now have our own centre, we call it The Hub and, we have 10 staff members. I am proud to say that 80 children and their families attend every week. During lockdown our group sizes were reduced drastically and we decided that every child should paint their favourite character on the wall of The Hub so that it truly became a place where they